Other Books by
RICHARD BRAUTIGAN

Novels

Trout Fishing in America
A Confederate General from Big Sur
In Watermelon Sugar
The Abortion: An Historical Romance 1966
The Hawkline Monster: A Gothic Western
Willard and His Bowling Trophies: A Perverse Mystery

Poetry

The Galilee Hitch-Hiker *
Lay the Marble Tea *
The Octopus Frontier *
All Watched Over by Machines of Loving Grace *
Please Plant This Book
The Pill Versus the Springhill Mine Disaster
Rommel Drives on Deep into Egypt

Short Stories

Revenge of the Lawn

* out of print

Sombrero Fallout
A Japanese Novel

Richard Brautigan

Simon and Schuster   New York

Published by Simon and Schuster
A Gulf+Western Company
Rockefeller Center, 630 Fifth Avenue
New York, New York 10020

Designed by Elizabeth Woll
Manufactured in the United States of America

1   2   3   4   5   6   7   8   9   10

Library of Congress Cataloging in Publication Data

Brautigan, Richard
  Sombrero fallout.

  I. Title.
PZ4.B826So   [PS3503.R2736]   813'.5'4   76-16137
ISBN 0-671-22331-3

This novel is for Junichirō Tanizaki who wrote The Key *and*
Diary of a Mad Old Man

Sombrero
Fallout

Sombrero

"A sombrero fell out of the sky and landed on the Main Street of town in front of the mayor, his cousin and a person out of work. The day was scrubbed clean by the desert air. The sky was blue. It was the blue of human eyes, waiting for something to happen. There was no reason for a sombrero to fall out of the sky. No airplane or helicopter was passing overhead and it was not a religious holiday."

The first tear formed itself in his right eye. That was the eye that always started crying first. Then the left followed. He would have found it interesting if he had known that the right eye started crying first. The left eye started crying so close after the right eye that he didn't know which eye started crying first, but it was always the right one.

He was very perceptive but he wasn't perceptive enough to know which eye started crying first. That is, if one can use such a small piece of information as any kind of definition of perception.

" 'Is that a sombrero?' the mayor said. Mayors always speak first, especially if it is impossible for them to rise to any other political position than mayor of a small town.

'Yes,' said his cousin, who wanted to be mayor himself.

The man who had no job said nothing. He waited to see which way the wind was blowing. He didn't want to rock the boat. Being out of work in America is no laughing matter.

'It fell from the sky,' said the mayor, looking up into the absolutely clear blue sky.

'Yes,' said his cousin.

The man who had no job said nothing because he wanted a job. He did not want to jeopardize whatever faint possibility he had of getting one. It was better for everybody if the big shots did all the talking.

The three men looked around for a reason for a sombrero to fall out of the sky but they couldn't find one, including the man who had no job.

The sombrero looked brand-new.

It was lying in the street with its crown pointed toward the sky.

Size: 7¼.

'Why are hats falling from the sky?' said the mayor.

'I don't know,' said his cousin.

The man who was without a job wondered if the hat would fit his head."

Now both eyes were crying.

Oh, God . . .

He reached into the typewriter as if he were an undertaker zipping up the fly of a dead man in his coffin and removed a piece of paper with everything that has been written here except for his crying, which he didn't know he was doing because he had done it so often recently that it was like drinking a glass of water that you drink accidentally when you are not thirsty and do not remember it afterwards.

He tore up the piece of paper that had everything that you have read here about the sombrero. He tore it up very carefully into many pieces and threw them on the floor.

He would start over again the next morning writing about something else that would have nothing to do with a sombrero falling out of the sky.

His business was writing books. He was a very well-known American humorist. It was difficult to find a bookstore that did not carry at least one of his titles.

Why was he crying, then?

Isn't fame enough?

The answer is quite simple.

His Japanese girlfriend was gone.

She had left him.

That was the reason for tears that started in eyes that he could no longer remember except for their crying which was now an everyday occurrence since the Japanese woman had left him.

Some days he cried so much that he thought that he was dreaming.

*J*apanese

As Yukiko slept, her hair slept long and Japanese about her. She didn't know that her hair was sleeping. Protein needs its rest, too. She did not think like that. Her thoughts were basically very simple.

She combed her hair in the morning.

It was the first thing that she did when she woke up. She always combed it very carefully. Sometimes she would put it in a bun on top of her head in the classic Japanese manner. Sometimes she would let it hang long, reaching to her ass.

It was a little after ten in the evening in San Francisco. Drops of Pacific rain fell against the window beside her bed, but she didn't hear them because she was sound asleep. She always slept very well and sometimes she would sleep for long periods of time: twelve hours or so, enjoying it as if she were actually doing something like going for a walk or cooking a good meal. She also liked to eat.

As he tore up the sheet of paper with words on it about a sombrero falling from the sky, she slept and her hair slept with her: long and dark next to her.

Her hair dreamt about being very carefully combed in the morning.

Ghost

He looked at the pieces of paper on the floor about a sombrero falling out of the sky for no apparent reason and somehow the sight of them increased his crying.

Who was she sleeping with? he thought, as his eyes raced with tears trying to get out, rushing all at once in front of one another, competing to get down his cheeks as if they were in an Olympiad of Crying with visions of gold medals in front of them.

He imagined her in bed with another man. The man he thought up to be her lover had no definite body or color of hair or even features. Her imaginary lover did not have bones, flesh or blood. The man he had placed in bed with her was just a ghost-like energy force with a penis.

He probably, if it's possible, would have cried even more if he had known she was sleeping alone. That would have made him feel even sadder.

Sailor

What was he going to do with the rest of the night? It was 10:15 in November. He didn't want to watch the eleven o'clock news. He wasn't hungry. He didn't want a drink. He knew if he tried to read a book the pages would swim through the tears in his eyes.

So he thought about her fucking somebody else. He thought about another man, a nameless face with his penis entering her. He thought about her moaning and moving under the weight of another man's cock. Thoughts like that were no good for him but he clung to them like a drowning sailor to a board in the middle of an ocean without horizons.

Then he looked down at the pieces of paper at his feet. Why should a sombrero fall out of the sky? The torn pieces of paper would never be able to tell him. He sat down on the floor in the middle of them.

*E*raser

The Japanese woman slept on.

Yukiko had gone to bed very tired. It had been a hard day for her. All she wanted to do at work was to go home and go to sleep, and now here she was: she was home sleeping.

She had a small dream about her childhood. It was a dream that she would not remember when she woke up in the morning nor would she ever remember it.

It was gone forever.

It was actually gone as she dreamt it.

It erased itself as it happened.

Breathing

The first time he met her he was very drunk one night in San Francisco. She had gotten off work and had gone to a bar with some co-workers. She didn't like to drink because typically Japanese she couldn't hold her liquor and besides that, she didn't really like the feeling of alcohol in her body. It made her feel dizzy.

So she didn't go to bars very often.

After she finished work that night she was tired but her two co-workers persuaded her to go with them to a local bar where young people hung out.

When he turned around on his bar stool, very drunk, which was a condition not unknown to him, and saw her sitting there in her uniform, little did he know that two years later he would be sitting on the floor surrounded by little pieces of paper dealing with a sombrero falling out of the sky, his eyes dashing tears forth like a spring creek in the mountains and he would have nowhere to go forever and his life would be tired of breathing him.

Suburb

Yukiko rolled over.
That plain, that simple.
Her body was small in its moving.
And her hair followed, dreaming her as she moved.

A cat, her cat, in bed with her was awakened by her moving, and watched her turn slowly over in bed. When she stopped moving, the cat went back to sleep.

It was a black cat and could have been a suburb of her hair.

Origami

He picked up the many torn pieces of paper about the sombrero and dropped them into an empty wastepaper basket which was dark and totally bottomless, but the pieces of white paper miraculously found a bottom and lay upon it glowing faintly upward like a reverse origami cradled on the abyss.

He did not know that she slept alone.

G_{irl}

There had to be a way out of this.

Then he knew what to do. He called a girl on the telephone. She was pleased that it was him when she answered the telephone. "I'm glad you called," she said. "Why don't you come over and have a nightcap with me? I'd like to see you."

She only lived four blocks away.

There was the sound of romance in her voice.

For years they had been on and off casual lovers and she was very good in bed. She had read all of his books and was very intelligent because she never talked to him about them. He didn't like to talk about his books and she had never asked him anything about them, but they were all there on her bookshelf. He liked the idea of her having all of his books but he liked even better the fact that they had been lovers for five years now and she had never asked him about them. He wrote them, she read them, and they did some pretty fair fucking together.

She wasn't his physical type but she compensated for it in other ways.

"I'd like to see you," she said on the telephone.

"I'll be over in a few minutes," he said.

"I'll put a log on the fire," she said.

He was feeling better now.

Maybe it would all work out.

Perhaps, it wasn't hopeless.

He put his coat on and started out the door.

Actually, he did nothing because he had been only thinking about all of this in his mind. None of it was real. He hadn't touched the telephone and there was no such girl.

He was still staring at the torn pieces of paper in the wastepaper basket. He was staring very intently at them as they made friends with the abyss. They seemed to have a life of their own. It was a big decision but they decided to go on without him.

Mayor

"Why are hats falling from the sky?" said the mayor.

"I don't know," said his cousin.

The man who was without a job wondered if the hat would fit his head.

"This is serious," said the mayor. "Let me take a look at that sombrero." He gestured toward the hat and his cousin immediately reached to pick it up because he wanted to be mayor himself someday and picking up that hat might get him some political help in the future when his name would be on the ballot.

The mayor might even endorse him and say at a big rally, "I've been a good mayor and you've re-elected me six times but I know my cousin here will be a great mayor and carry on a tradition of honesty and leadership in our community."

Yes, it was a very good idea to pick up the sombrero.

His future as mayor depended on it.

He would have been an idiot if he'd said, "Pick it up yourself. Who do you think you are, anyway? I wasn't put on this earth to pick up sombreros for you."

Berries

Though it was a hot day, the sombrero was ice-cold. When the cousin touched the hat, he withdrew his hand immediately as if he had touched electricity.

"What's wrong?" said the mayor.

"This sombrero is cold," his cousin said.

"What?" the mayor said.

"It's cold."

"Cold?"

"Ice-cold."

The man who did not have a job stared at the sombrero. It didn't look cold to him. But what did he know? He didn't have a job. Perhaps if he had a job the sombrero would have looked cold to him. Maybe that's why he didn't have a job. He couldn't see a cold sombrero when he was looking at one.

His unemployment benefits had run out a month before

and he was now reduced to eating berries that he found growing in the nearby foothills.

He was very tired of eating berries.

He wanted a hamburger.

*H*amburgers

An idea took immediate form in the unemployed man's mind. The sombrero was still lying in the street. The mayor's cousin had failed to pick it up. He had jumped back as if he'd been stung by a bee when he tried to pick it up.

The sombrero lay there.

Perhaps if the unemployed man picked up the sombrero and handed it to the mayor, the mayor would give him a job and he could stop eating berries and eat a lot of hamburgers instead.

He looked again at the sombrero lying in the street and his mouth started watering at the imagined taste of hamburgers with lots of onions and catsup on them.

He would not let this chance go by.

He might never be employed again if he did not pick up that sombrero and hand it to the mayor.

What was he going to do when the berry season was over?

What a terrible thought.

No more berries.

Even though he hated berries now, they were better to eat than nothing. What was he going to do when they were gone?

This sombrero lying in the street might be his last chance.

Career

"I'll get the sombrero for you, mayor," he said and bent over to pick up the sombrero.

"No, I'll get it," the mayor's cousin said, suddenly realizing that if he didn't pick up that sombrero he might never be mayor.

Who was this unemployed bastard who was trying to pick up the sombrero and ruin his bid for public office? Did he want to become mayor himself? Even if the sombrero was frighteningly cold, he wasn't going to let this son-of-a-bitch pick it up and become mayor of the town.

Why didn't I just pick it up in the first place? the cousin thought. Then none of this would be happening. An ice-cold sombrero can't hurt you. It just surprised him. That was all. He didn't expect it to be cold, so he had jumped back. Who would have thought that the sombrero would be frozen? Anyone would have been surprised and reacted the way he did.

Suddenly the cousin hated the sombrero for having made a fool out of him. He had to hand that sombrero to the mayor if he ever wanted to be mayor himself. His whole political career would end right then and there if he didn't get the sombrero to the mayor.

God-damn sombrero!

*J*ob

When the unemployed man saw that the mayor's cousin was suddenly very anxious to pick up the sombrero, he panicked. He knew for certain that he would never get a job again if he didn't get that sombrero to the mayor.

Why did the mayor's cousin want to pick up the sombrero?

He already had a job.

His hands weren't covered with berry stains.

*B*room

The heart-broken American humorist of course had no idea what was going on among the torn pieces of paper in his wastepaper basket. He did not know that they now had a life of their own and had gone on without him. He grieved only for his lost Japanese love. He thought about calling her up on the telephone and telling her that he loved her and would do anything in this world to have her back again.

He looked at the telephone.

She was only seven numbers away from him.

All he had to do was dial them.

Then he would hear her voice.

It would be very sleepy because he would have awakened her. It would sound as if it were coming from a great distance. Perhaps Kyoto, though she was only a mile away in the Richmond District of San Francisco.

"Hello," she said.

"It's me. Can you talk?"

"No, somebody's here with me. It's over between us. Don't call again. It irritates him when you call."

"What?"

"The man I'm in love with. He doesn't like it when you call. So don't call any more. OK?"

click

Then she hung up.

While she was hanging up in his mind, she slept alone with her cat beside her in bed. She was sound asleep. She had gone to bed with no one since they had broken up a month ago. She hadn't even gone out on a date with another man. All she did was work at her job, come home and do needlework or read. She was reading Proust. She didn't know why. Sometimes she visited her brother and his wife and they would all watch television together.

It had been a very uneventful time for her since she had broken up with the American humorist. She had been thinking a lot about her life while she was doing these other things. She was twenty-six years old and she was trying to put it into perspective. Somewhere during the two years she had gone out with the humorist, she had lost the dimensions of her existence and what she wanted out of life. The humorist had taken an enormous amount of energy from her. She constantly had to feed his insecurity and neurosis with her security and mental stability. After two years of this, she didn't know who she was any more. In the beginning all she had wanted out of life was to live with him, have children and enjoy a normal existence.

His basic insanity stopped any of this from becoming a reality.

After about a year together she realized that loving him

was not good for her but it took another year for her to end it and now she was very glad that it was over.

Sometimes she wondered how she had allowed it to go on for such a long time.

I will be very careful the next time I fall in love, she told herself. Also, she had made a promise to herself that she intended on keeping. She was never going to go out with another writer: no matter how charming, sensitive, inventive or fun they could be. They weren't worth it in the long run. They were emotionally too expensive and the upkeep was too complicated. They were like having a vacuum cleaner around that broke all the time and only Einstein could fix it.

She wanted her next lover to be a broom.

Bar

He looked at the clock. It was 10:30. He could not call her on the telephone because he knew that she was with another man: enjoying his body, moaning softly underneath him . . . and loving him.

A huge sigh hurricaned his body and then he sat down on the couch. He tried to sort it all out. She was a thousand pieces of a puzzle tumbling around in his mind as if they were in a dryer in a Laundromat.

For a few moments his mind was simultaneously the past, the present and the future, and there was no form to his thoughts about her. Then her hair began to emerge as a dominant theme in his grief. He had always loved her hair. It was somewhat of an obsession with him. Thoughts of her hair, how long and dark and hypnotic it was, began to put pieces of the puzzle together until he was remembering the first time he met her

Two years ago, it was raining.

She didn't go to bars very often.

After she finished work that evening she was tired but her two co-workers persuaded her to go with them to a local bar where young people hung out.

He was there and he was very bored. He was often very bored and he did not think twice about telling other people about his boredom. He bore it with the good humor of a cross.

When he turned around on his bar stool, very drunk, which was a condition not unknown to him, he saw her sitting at a table with two other women. They were all wearing white uniforms. They looked as if they had just gotten off work.

She was beautiful.

Her hair was combed into a bun on top of her head in the classic Japanese style. The drink in front of her had barely been touched. She was listening to the other women talk. One of them was talking a lot and enjoying the drink in front of her.

The Asian woman was very quiet.

He stared at her and she looked back for a few seconds and then returned to listening to the women talk.

He wondered if she had recognized him. Sometimes women did and it was to his advantage. His books were popular and easily obtained in bookstores.

He turned back to the bar and ordered another drink. He would have to think this one over. He was a very shy person when he was sober. He had to be drunk before he could make a pass at a woman. As he sipped his drink, he wondered if he was drunk enough to go over to the table where the Asian woman was sitting and try to get to know her. He turned around again to look at her but she was already looking at him. It rattled him and he turned back around again to the bar and his ears were burning with embarrassment.

No, he was not drunk enough to make a pass at her.

He motioned to the bartender who came over.

"Another one?" the bartender said, looking at the one that was only half-empty in front of him.

"A double," he said.

The bartender's face remained expressionless because he was a very good bartender. He went and got the whiskey. By the time he was back, the humorist had finished the glass that had been half-full. A minute later the double was half-gone. The humorist with two sips had changed it into a single.

He could feel the Asian woman looking at him.

She's read my books, he thought.

Then he drained the glass in front of him.

It was as if the whiskey had fallen into a bottomless well without making a sound. Its only presence now was the energy for him to get up and walk over to the table where the woman sat and say, "Hello, may I join you?"

Breathing

The other two women stopped talking and looked up at him.

The Asian woman was very carefully looking at him.

He'd never had an Asian woman look that carefully at him before. Her eyes were dark and narrow. For a second because her eyes were so narrow he wondered if she could see as much as a Caucasian could. The thought vanished upon the thinking of it but it was to return many times during the two years that he knew her. It was just that he wondered sometimes if she could see everything that was in a room or wherever they were. Maybe she was only seeing 75 percent of what was going on.

It was the kind of thought that a child would have.

He'd never had any experience with an Asian woman other than just seeing them around San Francisco: Chinatown, Japantown, etc. He'd never had one of them look very carefully at him. There was also something else in her eyes that he had seen before in the eyes of other women when they looked at him.

He knew what it was.

He relaxed slightly.

"Please do," she said.

Then he sat down.

He knew by the expression in her eyes that everything was going to work out. Her breathing had changed slightly. She was breathing a little faster. The increase in her breathing pleased him.

The cocktail waitress came over and he ordered a round of drinks. Then they exchanged names at the table.

She was Japanese.

*H*umor

The other two women didn't like him.

They hadn't read his books. That made a big difference in meeting him. He was not a good-looking man. He had an attractive but very erratic personality. He allowed his moods to dominate him and they were very changeable. Sometimes he would talk too much and at other times he wouldn't talk at all. He always talked too much when he drank. When he wasn't drinking he was very shy and formal around people and it was hard to get to know him. Some people thought that he was very charming and others thought that he was a total asshole. The truth lay somewhere in between and it was very close to the halfway mark.

He had a national reputation as a humorist which was very funny in itself because when you met him one of the first things you noticed about him was that he had no sense of humor.

Whenever other people were laughing at something, he usually looked puzzled. Sometimes very intelligent people thought this was very funny in itself and got a second laugh after the first which would always make him look more puzzled and then he would feel very uncomfortable. He was very perceptive but that was one of the things in life that he could never figure out. It never dawned on him that people were laughing at him because he had no sense of humor. He thought that he was a very funny fellow because the books he wrote were funny. He didn't know that around other people he often looked puzzled when they were laughing. Intellectually he was able to dismiss this by thinking that other people were laughing at an in-joke.

Not having a sense of humor was one of the main character weaknesses that he possessed. He would have enjoyed life a little more if he had been able to laugh at it.

Oh, yes: another interesting thing: When he was writing things that later on people would praise as some of the best humor of the century, he didn't laugh when he wrote them. He didn't even smile.

The other two women didn't like him.

Good for them.

Too bad for the Japanese woman.

She liked him.

Future

"I'll get the sombrero for you, mayor," the un-employed man said and bent over to pick up the sombrero. It was his last chance to get a job on this planet and he did not believe in God. It was nothing personal but he just knew that there was no employment waiting for him in heaven because there was no heaven.

This sombrero lying in the street was his final hope.

"No, I'll get it," the mayor's cousin said, suddenly real-izing that if he didn't pick up the sombrero he would never be mayor. He would have no political career. The Presi-dency of the United States would be beyond his reach. He would never rub elbows with bigwigs in Washington nor give the Fourth of July speech here in town.

The sombrero was the key to his entire future.

The mayor was amused by the sudden intensity of the two men wanting to please him, though he didn't know what their reasons were. The mayor was a great small-town politician.

"No!" the unemployed man yelled. "I'll get the sombrero!"

"Don't touch that sombrero!" the cousin yelled back.

Both men who were reaching for the sombrero suddenly stopped, surprised by their own vehemence, and took a good look at each other.

The mayor was about to say, "Stop it, you two. What's wrong with you? Are you both idiots? It is only a sombrero."

That would have ended it right then and there. Life is that simple and the National Guard would not have to have been called out nor paratroopers and tanks brought in, along with Air Force support. There would not have been that speech the President gave on television condemning the activity that was to happen nor would the United States have been denounced in the United Nations by a special committee of Third World countries.

Most of all there would not have been the world-wide alert between the United States of America and the Union of Soviet Socialist Republics.

Yes, the world would not have been on the very brink of nuclear holocaust if the mayor had said, "It's only a sombrero. Stand back. I'll pick it up even if it is ice-cold. A sombrero can't hurt you."

L_{ock}

An hour later the American humorist was so nervous that he could not open the front door to his apartment with the key. He was so nervous that he was almost sober. He couldn't believe this beautiful Japanese woman was standing beside him in the hall of his apartment house, waiting for him to open the door and then to go inside his apartment with him.

She stood there very patiently watching him.

There was something wrong with the lock.

He couldn't believe it.

God-damn fucking lock! Why now? Why me!

This had never happened before.

"It's the lock," he said, fumbling with the key out of proportion to the actual situation.

She didn't say anything. That made it worse. He wished that she would say something. He didn't know then that the only time she ever said anything was when she had a specific thing to say. Then she was direct and very articulate. She never made small talk.

She was very intelligent, though, and had a great sense of humor but she just didn't talk very much. When other people were around, it always surprised them because she could go through an entire evening without saying a word. She only talked when she had something to say. She would listen very intelligently, nodding or shaking her head when subtle, intelligent points were made. She always laughed at precisely the right times.

She had a beautiful laugh which was like rain water pouring over daffodils made from silver. People liked to say funny things around her because her laughter was so attractive.

When other people were talking, she stared directly at them with very narrow understanding eyes that listened to them as if they were the only sound left in the world, as if everything else that made sound had disappeared entirely from the human ear and their voice was all there was left.

Without saying a word, she gently took the key out of his hand. It was the first time they had ever touched which was the slightest gesture of a key exchanging hands. Her hand was small but had long slender fingers. There was a tremendous calm to her hands.

He had not touched her in the bar or on their way over to his apartment. This was the first of a million touches. She put the key softly and precisely into the lock. She turned the key. The door opened. She handed the key back to him and they touched hands for the second time. He thought that his heart would pound its way out of his body. This was the most erotic thing that had ever happened to him.

For a brief time after they had broken up he went through

a period of masturbation. He used the image of her wordlessly taking the key from his hand and opening the door and then putting the key back in his hand as the theme for his masturbation.

He would come when she put the key back in his hand after having opened the door. Then he would be lying there in bed with a puddle of sperm floating on his stomach like a strange Sargasso Sea. He did this five or six times. Then he gave it up because he realized that he could go on doing it indefinitely and it would be the end of him. He knew that life did not have a happy ending but he did not want to finish his that way.

It would be better for him if he blew his brains out rather than having his life be completed in the form of a masturbating shoji panel.

He spent one night crying hour after hour because he wanted to masturbate. He wanted to masturbate to her taking the key away, unlocking the door and then returning the key to him more than anything else in this world. Finally, he was exhausted from crying but he didn't masturbate. He had to stop no matter how much it hurt him because it would be the end of him. Once during his crying he had a vision of what his tombstone would look like if he didn't stop masturbating to the touch of her hand, the remembered taking and returning of a key:

An American Humorist
1934–2009
Rest in Peace
He's Not Jacking Off Anymore.

Apartment

"You have a nice apartment," she said. She said it as if it meant something very important. It surprised him. He took another look at his apartment to see if he had missed anything during the five years he had lived there, but it looked just the same to him.

"Thank you," he said.

She didn't say anything else and sat down on the couch.

He thought that she was going to say something else. He had no reason to think this, but he did, anyway. He wasted a lot of time thinking about things that never came to anything. Often his mind turned into a popcorn popper over the simplest of things.

She didn't say a word.

He looked at her mouth. It was small and delicate as were all of her features. Her skin was almost white. Some Japanese people have very pale complexions. She was one of them. Again he wondered if she could see everything in the room through those very narrow eyes.

She could.

Then he asked her a question that he already knew the answer to but he asked it, anyway, because it gave him confidence in dealing with women when he asked them the question and they answered it the way he knew they would.

"Have you read any of my books?"

He waited for her to say yes. He could hear her voice in his mind saying yes. She had a very musical voice. It would please him when she said yes. Then he would have more confidence.

When she gave a very short but graceful nod of her head, not taking her eyes off him, he turned completely blank. That was the last thing in the world he had expected her to do. He had no backup mechanism to deal with it. He just stood there staring at her. All thoughts had fled his mind like robbers running out of a bank in the Depression. During the time that he stood there before anything else happened, he thought that ten years had passed.

She took one of her hands that had been folded in repose in her lap and reached up and touched a long white finger to her chin. The expression on her face did not change. The finger just brushed her chin and then her hand was back in her lap again.

She had not taken her eyes off him since she had sat down on the couch.

He hadn't had a woman look at him that long before. He was not a good-looking man but the way she looked at him somehow made him feel that he was.

Inches

"I'll pick the sombrero up," said the mayor, finally, but it was too late.

"NO!" the mayor's cousin and the unemployed man said in one voice to the mayor. Under no condition did they want the mayor to pick up the sombrero. That would be the end of both their careers. If the mayor touched that sombrero, their lives would be hopeless from that point on. Their futures would be gone. One of the men would never be mayor and the other man would never find a job again.

"I'll get the sombrero for you, your Excellency," his cousin said. "I wouldn't think of you bending over and picking up that hat. I'll do it. After all, you are our esteemed mayor. You shouldn't do things like that. You have more important business."

His cousin had launched into a speech.

Perhaps he would be a good mayor and might make a fine

President of the United States and be ranked by historians somewhere between Thomas Jefferson and Harry Truman. Yes, the man definitely had prospects.

Unfortunately, he had taken his eyes off the unemployed man who was slowly maneuvering himself an inch at a time toward the sombrero. Before the cousin started making his speech they were both about an equal distance to the sombrero. Now the unemployed man had gained an advantage of about nine inches closer.

The mayor's cousin needed a campaign manager to look after his interests while he was giving speeches. In a situation like this one it's important not to lose nine inches of your future. Of course rhetoric is important but not if you lose territory in its place. It is not an equal exchange if your whole future depends on picking up a sombrero and you have lost nine inches while you are talking.

Books

"I like your books," she said. "But you already know that."

He was stunned. He stood there looking at her. He waited for her to say something else. She didn't. She just smiled. Her smile was so subtle that it would have made the Mona Lisa seem like a clown performing a pratfall.

"Would you like a drink?" he said, suddenly pulling out of his psychic nose dive. Without waiting for her to answer he went into the kitchen and got a bottle of brandy and two glasses. It took him a few extra moments to get the brandy because he stood there in the kitchen, trying to figure out his next move.

He wanted very much to go to bed with this quiet and beautiful Japanese woman who miraculously was sitting on the couch in his apartment. It was something that he imagined would never happen. How was he going to succeed with her? He thought of her seduction as an exotic puzzle.

The pieces were floating like clouds across his mind but he couldn't even put two of them together. What was he going to do?

Suddenly he was very depressed, a feeling of hopelessness replaced the clouds in his mind. He sighed and walked back into the room.

The Japanese woman had taken her shoes and socks off and was sitting on the couch with her legs gracefully folded in a sort of meditating position that had a sensual quality. It was as if sensuality had brushed her body like a gentle summer breeze.

He was not prepared to see her sitting there with her shoes and socks off in that position. It was the last thing in the world he expected. Just a few seconds before in the kitchen his thoughts of seducing her had all turned to despair.

When he saw her there on the couch it completely turned his mind around and he was instantaneously relaxed. All thoughts of seduction had disappeared. He was very calm. He put the bottle of brandy and the two glasses down on a table. He did not pour himself or her a drink. He just left the bottle and glasses alone on the table and he walked over to the couch and sat down beside her and reached out and took her hand which was reaching toward him.

He held her hand softly in his hand.

He looked very carefully at her fingers as if he had never seen fingers before. He was enchanted by them and thought that they were beautiful. He never wanted to let go. He wanted to hold her hand forever.

Her hand tightened in his hand.

He looked from her hand to her eyes.

They were narrow dark spaces filled with a reaching soft-
ness.

"You don't have to do anything," she said. Her voice,
delicate as it was, had a strength to it that made one realize
why a teacup can stay in one piece for centuries, defying the
changes of history and the turmoil of man.

"I'm sorry," he said.

She smiled again and looked beyond his face to the room
where his bed was. Without saying anything more he got up
and led her there. Though he walked slightly in front of her,
holding her hand, she was really the guide.

Asleep

They stopped in front of his bed and he let go of her hand. They stood there for a few seconds, looking at the bed as if it were a door and of course it was a door, the door to a house filled with many rooms that they would explore over a two-year period.

The last room in the house would be her sleeping alone this evening, never wanting to see him again, with her hair lying beside her dreaming worlds of its own, echoing existences totally composed of protein where our souls have a different dimension and serve a different purpose.

Then this small Japanese woman turned in her sleep but it was more a drifting motion than a turning one. Her sleep movement was like an apple blossom fluttering to the ground in early May through absolutely still air. Nothing moves except the blossom that stops moving when it touches the earth.

It lies there like a flower that came from the ground instead of the sky.

Her cat beside her purred for a few seconds, then forgot why it was purring and stopped.

700,000 people lived in San Francisco.

Maybe 350,000 of them were asleep now.

Their sleep demanded this much attention.

They would never get it.

*F*uneral

After standing there looking at the bed she reached up and let her hair down. It was held in place by a golden barrette of Japanese origin. Her neck was long and white, curving forward like a delicate movement of alabaster.

The American humorist watched her let her hair down.

When she unfastened the barrette, her hair tumbled backward like total night and plunged the back of her neck into darkness.

Her hair was very long and reached almost down to the belt that was around the waist of her white uniform. The belt was also white. Her clothes matched the paleness of her skin.

Her physical presence was like a meeting place between day and night where day was the majority and night's minority was her narrow eyes and her midnight starless hair.

She turned and reached up like dew on early morning grass and took his face in her hands and led it sweetly down until their mouths were touching.

Then her hands fell away from his face and settled like pioneers on his hips.

He thought his heart would stop.

His own funeral flashed across his mind.

It would be a nice one.

He saw this beautiful Japanese woman at the funeral, wearing a veil that matched her eyes.

She was walking in front of his coffin as it was being carried to the grave. She moved in perfect rhythm with the pallbearers and the coffin. His funeral flowed like a river into eternity.

There was no stopping.

They moved past his grave.

They did not stop for that open hole.

They continued on with her leading the way forever.

Winter

Suddenly the mayor's cousin slammed on the brakes to his speech because he realized as he was making good verbal points with the mayor, the unemployed man had been inching closer to the sombrero.

"Where are you going?" he said to his sombrero opponent. "Where in the hell do you think you're going?"

"I need a job!" the unemployed man yelled. "I can't live on berries forever! Winter is coming! I want a hamburger!"

"My fine friends," the mayor said as he perceived that the pot was ready to boil over. "What is the matter?"

Both men took a huge step toward the sombero and were on their way toward taking another step when the mayor yelled, "Stop it!"

Both men stopped it.

There would be no point in getting the sombrero for the mayor if the mayor was mad at them. All would be lost, then. One of them would not become President of the United States and the other one would remain unemployed forever. That's a lot of berries to eat. It was important that giving the sombrero to the mayor should please him.

Both men's feet were now glued to the ground. They weren't going anywhere. They waited for further developments. The mayor had them in the palm of his hand.

"It's only a sombrero," the mayor said, his voice becoming quieter and taking on a patronizing tone. "It's only a sombrero," he repeated, almost whispering. "I can pick it up myself."

His cousin looked as if he had been slapped across the face by a shark.

Good-bye, Presidency.

Tears started to form in the unemployed man's eyes.

Good-bye, job.

Crying

"Let us be reasonable men," the mayor said softly. "Let us discuss this in a manner befitting reasonable men," the mayor said patronizingly to the two men who were both crying now, blubbering away like babies. They had lost all composure when they saw their ambitions starting to vanish.

"After all, it is only a sombrero that has fallen from the sky," the mayor said sweetly. "Anyone can pick it up. Picking it up is no big deal. Now I want to know why you are crying. What has driven two strong men like you to tears? Tell me. I am your mayor. I have been mayor for six terms. I can help you. I may be the only person who can. Let me hear what it is. Do not spare a single detail. After you have told me everything you will feel better."

Both men just stood there crying.

They had lost the power of speech.

Their minds had been overpowered by despair.

They had been turned into shadows of themselves.

The human mind can only handle so much.

Then it stops.

"Speak up," said the mayor. "Stop crying and tell me what the problem is. Why are you acting this way? I know it has something to do with picking up the sombrero but you have to tell me what it is. I am not a mind reader." When the mayor said that he was not a mind reader his voice suddenly grew loud and had an angry tone to it. This did not help the situation at all.

The two men only cried louder.

"I am your mayor!" the mayor shouted at the bawling men.

Black

It appears now that the relating of these sombrero events needs to be interrupted for a closer examination of the sombrero. The only things known about the sombrero so far are:

1. It fell out of the sky.
2. It is size 7¼.
3. It is very cold.

Here are a few more details about the sombrero that should be of some use:

4. The sombrero is black. (Interesting that this fact had not been brought up until now.)
5. It is known that the sombrero is very cold but the exact temperature has not been revealed before. Here it is: The temperature of the sombrero is 24 degrees below zero.

That's a cold sombrero.

Especially when the temperature in the street is 81 and

the sombrero's temperature stays at 24 below. It is not affected by the sun.

That makes it a very different sombrero.

That's enough for now and the two men still haven't stopped crying and of course a crowd is starting to gather but you knew that was going to happen sooner or later, so it is no surprise that they are now leaving their houses and stores and starting toward the three men and the sombrero in the street.

The tempo is now changing.

In just a short while this chapter will be looked back upon as the good old days when men loved one another and peace reigned on earth.

Clothes

    After his funeral, they took their clothes off and got into bed. They took their clothes off in response to an invisible signal. Nothing was said nor was there a gesture made but something happened between them that caused them to just start taking their clothes off at exactly the same time.

A fourth-dimensional exchange had been made between them and the beginning of their love-making, two years of it, was set into motion.

She took her clothes off like a kite takes gently to a warm April wind. He fumbled his clothes off like a football game being played in November mud.

He had never been very good at taking his clothes off and for that matter, putting them on. He was also one of those people who have a lot of trouble drying themselves after a

66

bath. When he was through drying himself, 50 percent of his body was always still wet.

While she was taking her clothes off, she watched him take his off and she wondered if he were that way in bed. She hoped not. She enjoyed making love and liked it done in a way that pleased her. She did not have much patience with men who were bad in bed.

Fortunately for him most of the time he was very good in bed. It always surprised women. It was one of his best personal traits.

Unfortunately for her it was to contribute to her more or less wasting two years of her life. Anyway, that's how she looked at it when it was over. Of course many times when it was going on she thought it was very good. The good times tended to vanish in retrospect when she examined them. She had poured two years of her life into him and more of her youth than she had intended.

After she took her clothes off, she slipped into bed and under the covers. She watched him standing there fumbling off the last of his clothes.

Interesting, she thought. One would never imagine this by reading his books. She already knew that he was going to be quite different from his books. She just hoped that he was going to be good in bed.

As was stated earlier, unfortunately for her, he was.

Revelation

Now two years later he had spent a whole evening suffering over her departure from his life. His grief was so intense that, after hours and hours of it, he was very hungry. He needed something to eat. He thought about going down to the corner where there was a hamburger stand but he changed his mind because he didn't want a hamburger. He had eaten two of them the day before and didn't want another one. Another hamburger right now was just too close to the burgers he'd had yesterday.

If I hadn't eaten those hamburgers yesterday, he thought, *I could have one now.*

Somehow this was a revelation to him that he immediately gave too much significance. That was a real problem for him. Too many things were out of proportion in his life in relationship to their real meaning.

Soon he found himself cursing the two burgers that he'd had yesterday.

I was a damn fool to eat those hamburgers, he thought. *What in the hell got into me? What was I thinking? Now I don't want a hamburger. If I hadn't eaten those burgers, I'd want one now.*

Shit!

Electricity

To some men the most beautiful sight in this world is a sleeping Japanese woman. The sight of her long black hair floating beside her like dark lilies makes them want to die and be transported to a paradise that is filled with sleeping Japanese women who never wake but sleep on for all time, dreaming beautiful dreams.

Yukiko could easily have been the queen of such a paradise and reigned perfectly and majestically over a million sleeping Japanese women from horizon to horizon.

Now this evening on Commonwealth Street in San Francisco she was the queen of her own sleep. Her breathing was slow and steady like the ticking of a clock in a castle.

She was dreaming a luxurious dream about Kyoto.

A warm autumn rain was falling in her dream. The rain was halfway between a mist and fine droplets. She had deliberately left her umbrella at home. She wanted to feel the rain touching her. She deliciously wanted to get slightly wet and this was what was happening and it made her feel very good.

If one had bent very quietly over her sleeping form until they got very close to her, they would have smelled a warm feminine delicately humid perfume drifting upward from her body that dreamed of walking through falling rain in Kyoto. Then one would have been tempted to reach down with their hand to see if there were tiny droplets of rain on her hair like diamonds of friendly electricity.

T*una*

After he had exhausted all thoughts of eating hamburgers, his mind entertained the possibility of a tuna fish sandwich but that was not a good idea. He always tried very hard not to think about tuna fish sandwiches. For the last three years he had been trying to keep thoughts of tuna fish sandwiches out of his mind. Whenever he thought about tuna fish sandwiches, he felt bad and now here he was thinking about a tuna fish sandwich again after he had tried so hard not to think about them.

There was a big tuna fish sandwich on white bread and very moist, almost dripping with mayonnaise, just the way he liked them, right in the middle of his mind with all his mental spotlights shining down on it, and immediately, as always was the case, he felt bad.

He tried to banish the tuna fish sandwich from his mind but it refused to leave. It clung there like a barnacle to an

Ethiopian battleship. The tuna fish sandwich wouldn't budge. He tried one more time to get the sandwich out of his mind but it just wouldn't move.

His feeling bad turned into simple despair.

He had to sit down.

All of this was because he loved tuna fish and hadn't had any for over three years. He used to average five tuna fish sandwiches a week and now he hadn't had any in years and his life felt barren sometimes without a tuna fish sandwich.

Often he would find himself unconsciously picking up a can of tuna in the supermarket before he realized what he had done. He would suddenly find himself halfway through reading the contents on the can before he knew what he was doing. Then he would look startled as if he had been caught reading a pornographic novel in church and quickly put the can back on the shelf and walk away from it, trying to forget that he had ever touched it.

Why did the American humorist have such a big problem with tuna fish? The answer is quite simple: fear. He was afraid of it. He was thirty-eight years old and afraid of tuna fish. It's that simple. The reason for the fear was mercury.

When they discovered a few years ago that there was more mercury in tuna fish than normal, he stopped eating it because he was afraid that it would accumulate in his brain and affect his thinking which would lead to an effect on his writing.

He thought his writing would get strange and nobody would buy his books because they had been corrupted by mercury and he would go crazy if he ate tuna fish, so he stopped eating it.

His decision to give up eating tuna fish sandwiches had been one of the most difficult and traumatic decisions that he had ever made. It still caused him to have bad dreams.

Once he even went to his doctor and asked him if there was enough mercury in tuna fish to hurt him. His doctor said, "No, eat tuna fish if you want to," but he still wouldn't eat tuna fish. He was afraid to follow his doctor's advice.

He really loved tuna but he loved his art even more, so he tried not to think about tuna fish sandwiches any more, but being human he slipped up sometimes which he had just done and his soul was paying the consequences.

He sat on the couch with his hands trembling from the opposite polarities of tuna fish sandwich attraction and fear.

One can only have profound sympathy for the sleeping Japanese woman a mile away in San Francisco. She had put up with two years of this kind of behavior and sometimes she put up with things that would make this seem like child's play. She had observed a never ending series of partially or fully developed raging obsessions and personality ambiguities that often made her work seem like the calmest part of her day.

She was a psychiatrist working in the emergency ward of a local hospital.

The nuts she had to deal with at night were simple uncomplicated folk compared to him.

Crowd

A small crowd had by now gathered around the mayor, the two crying men and the sombrero. The people were curious as to what was up but they just stood around watching the mayor, the two crying men and the sombrero.

The crowd wasn't talking very much. Every once in a while there would be a little whispering going on. One would be hard put to imagine that these same people would soon be overwhelming the local police, fighting the National Guard to a standstill and then taking on paratroopers, tanks and helicopter gunships. There was absolutely no way of knowing this by looking at them right now.

The mayor continued trying to make the two men stop crying, so that he could get to the bottom of it all but the two men's minds were drowning in a waterfall of tears and they were unable to stop crying or to explain themselves.

The crowd continued whispering:

"*Is that a sombrero?*" one of them whispered.

"*That is a sombrero,*" came a whisper back.

"*What's it doing in the street?*"

"*I don't know. I just got here myself.*"

"*Does it belong to somebody?*"

"*I don't know.*"

"*Neither do I.*"

"*I know you don't know because you just asked me.*"

"*That's right. I did. I'm sorry.*"

"*There's nothing to be sorry about.*"

"*Thank you.*"

There was more whispering on the other side of the crowd:

"*Why are they crying?*"

"*Is that the mayor's cousin?*"

"*Yes.*"

"*Why is he crying? I've never seen him cry before. He's never been a cry baby. I went to high school with him. He was on the track team. He ran the 100 in 10.3. Damn good runner. Never cried.*"

"*Quiet! I want to hear what the mayor's saying.*"

"*10.3 was a good time in those days.*"

"*That's fine but I want to hear the mayor.*"

"*Have I been talking too much?*"

"*Yes!*"

The mayor was becoming very exasperated:

"STOP CRYING!" he shouted. "STOP IT THIS VERY INSTANT! DO YOU HEAR ME? I AM YOUR MAYOR! I ORDER THAT YOU STOP CRYING!"

The mayor's yelling only insured the fact that the two men would continue crying and start crying even harder if that were possible and it turned out that it was.

The whispering continued:

"Why is the mayor yelling? I've never heard him yell before."

"I don't know. I voted for the other candidate. Did you vote for the mayor?"

"Yeah, I voted for him."

"Then don't ask me why he's yelling. You voted for him."

Two women started whispering:

"It's scandalous."

"What's scandalous?"

"This."

"Oh."

Children were whispering:

"These men are crying."

"Yeah, they're worse than we are."

"If I cried like that, I'd have to go to my room."

Old people were whispering:

"Did you hear about the increase we're getting in Social Security?"

"No, I didn't."

"4.1 percent starting in November if the Congress approves it."

"What if they don't approve it?"

"What?"

"I said: What if the Congress doesn't approve it?"

Two housewives were whispering:

"My period's eight days overdue."

"Do you think you're pregnant again?"

"I hope not. Three kids are enough."

"I remember when you said that you wanted to have an even dozen."

"I was out of my mind, then."

The whispering gathered in momentum.

The crowd was becoming larger and more active.

The whispering suddenly sounded like a hive of bees.

They were proceeding on schedule step by step down the path that would end up with them battling Federal troops and cause their small town to be plunged into world focus.

It wouldn't be long now.

It was only a matter of hours before the sound of machine gun and artillery fire would be very familiar to their ears and the whole world would be watching.

They were only a few days away from the President of the United States arriving there to survey the damage and to extend the healing palm frond of consolation and reconciliation.

He would also make that famous speech that was to be judged favorably with Lincoln's Gettysburg Address. In a few years it would be printed in high school textbooks. There would also be a national holiday declared to honor the dead and rededicate the living to the cause of national unity.

Avocado

       Finally the tuna-fish-sandwich vision vanished from his mind and he was able to use his intelligence to search further for something to eat because by now he was very hungry. He needed something to eat and quick.

The feeling of tuna-fish-sandwich despair was gone and his mind played with other nutritional possibilities. There had to be something that he could eat.

Burgers were out and so were tuna sandwiches.

That left thousands of other things to eat and he thought about some of them.

He did not want soup.

He had a can of mushroom soup in the kitchen but he wasn't going to eat it.

No way.

He thought about an avocado.

That would be good.

I'll have an avocado.

He mentally tasted a bite of avocado with lemon juice and it tasted good. Yes, an avocado would be the thing. Then he remembered that he did not have an avocado and all the stores near his apartment were closed because it was late in the evening.

He'd bought an avocado a month before on the day that the Japanese woman had told him that she no longer wanted to see him. He was so emotionally upset that he ignored the avocado and eventually it rotted on a kitchen windowsill and he had to throw it out.

He wished that he had that avocado now. He would put some lemon juice on it and his hunger would be taken care of. Then he would have something else to worry about. He could return to thinking about his love for the lost Japanese woman or he could occupy his mind with some chicken shit thing of no significance. He never lacked things to worry about. They followed him around like millions of trained white mice and he was their master. If he taught all his worries to sing, they would have made the Mormon Tabernacle Choir sound like a potato.

Maybe some scrambled eggs, he thought, though he knew there were no eggs in the house and he had no intention of going out to a restaurant.

Yes, some eggs would be fine.

Light and fluffy.

That's it.

Eggs.

Seattle

Often during Yukiko's two-year affair with him she would be with him at this hour of the night. When she got off work around ten, she would go over to his apartment and spend the night with him.

After spending eight hours with psychologically disturbed people, suicide attempts, nervous breakdowns or just plain crazy, she got to share his mental goodies.

An interesting thing is that she never classified or thought of him in terms of her patients. She never related him to them. She just thought of him as a genre complete in himself: one of a kind. Also, she was in love with him, so she did not have any objectivity toward his rollercoaster mind.

Shortly after meeting him she reread all his books to make sure that her recollections of them were accurate. When she had read the books before meeting him, she thought that the books were about him, that he was the main character in them and he wrote about himself.

When she reread the books she saw very little of his real personality in them. She wondered how he could so artfully conceal his real personality from his readers. It bordered on genius. This man was so complicated that he could make a labyrinth seem like a straight line. In the beginning she found it attractive because she was very intelligent. By the time it began to bother her, it was too late: She was in love with him and as things got worse she fell deeper and deeper in love with him.

She wasn't a masochist either.

It just went that way.

During the month that they were no longer seeing each other, a lot of things fell into perspective for her. She thought about why she had gone on seeing him and sorted through tons of brain garbage to come up with some conclusions that had the ring of objectivity to them. They were all fairly elementary things that she could easily have ferreted out of one of her patients but she had been unable to see them because she was in love with him.

Here are some of the things she thought about:

1. There was never a dull moment with him, even when he was stark-raving mad. Her patients' antics would often bore her because they were so predictable. His problems were unique and his ability to create new obsessions was awesome.

2. Often he was very kind and considerate and would do all sorts of little things to please her.

3. The most important thing was his ability to please her in bed. He was a wonderful lay. If he had been 50 percent less good in bed, she would have been free of him much earlier. Their affair would have lasted only a few months.

Two years is a long time.

She had a lot to think about but she was asleep now and her mind was doing other things. It was dreaming of Japan.

Yukiko was born in Tokyo but her parents moved to America when she was six months old. Her father was a diplomat and she was raised in America with a trip to Japan every two years. Her parents taught her both Japanese and English but because of growing up in Seattle, Washington, Japanese became her second language.

When she was fourteen her mother became an adulteress by having an affair with a high official at the Boeing aircraft plant in Seattle. When her father found out about the affair, he responded to it by committing suicide in his office. Her father had been an officer in the Japanese Imperial Army during World War II and he was a very honorable man. He killed himself by committing hara-kiri with a letter opener.

The event was well covered by the media. There was an article about it in *Life* magazine and it was on the eleven o'clock news. All of the networks had something to say about it.

Her father's body was cremated and shipped back to Japan and the Boeing executive left his wife of twenty-two years and married Yukiko's mother and she lived with them.

Seattle was rocked by the scandal because the executive had political aspirations and had been receiving a lot of encouragement.

Yukiko didn't care much for her stepfather but she stayed at home until she graduated from the University of Washington. She loved her mother very much, so her stepfather never knew that she didn't like him. She even tolerated his nickname for her. He called her "China Doll."

She did her psychiatric graduate work at UCLA and then moved to San Francisco where she did her internship and was now working at night in the emergency ward in one of the city's hospitals.

Yukiko had been to Japan nine times for brief stays and now she was dreaming of warm autumn rain in Kyoto which was her favorite city.

She had deliberately left her umbrella at her aunt's house and was joyed by the touch of the rain against her face and her hair.

She was on her way to the cemetery where her father's ashes were buried. Normally, she felt sad when she went to his grave but today she didn't. The rain made her happy.

She knew that he would understand.

R*iot*

Meanwhile back in the wastepaper basket—

"I AM YOUR MAYOR! SHOW ME SOME RESPECT!
I ORDER YOU TO STOP CRYING! I'LL CALL THE
POLICE!" the mayor shouted at the two crying men. He
was at the end of his rope. He couldn't deal with the
situation rationally any more. The crowd was quite large by
now and the mayor had gone off his rocker.

"POLICE! POLICE! POLICE!" he shouted, though one
of the crying men was his own cousin. The mayor had had
it. He was going mad.

The police of course were on their way. Somebody had
telephoned them as soon as the mayor went mad and told
them that there was a full-scale riot on Main Street.

"Bring lots of tear gas!" the person said over the telephone. The person was a little hysterical, so the police didn't know what to think, but they were on their way.

In the midst of the two men crying and the mayor shouting and the sombrero just lying there, the crowd had become very agitated. They were no longer whispering. They were talking in loud conversational tones and some of them had started shouting themselves:

"What is happening?"

"I don't know!"

"I'm afraid!" an old man shouted.

"This is ridiculous!" a teen-age girl shouted.

"The mayor is crazy!" a middle-aged woman shouted, just barely getting the words out before somebody punched her in the mouth. It was a good blow and knocked her to the street. She was out like a light.

The person who punched her had voted for the mayor in every election he had run in and could not stand to hear his beloved mayor spoken of in such terms. The man did not get to enjoy his revenge for very long because just about as soon as the woman hit the street with a solid unconscious thud, the man was rendered unconscious himself by a much larger man.

There are still some men left who will not stand around and watch a woman punched into oblivion. They don't care what circumstances motivated the knockout blow. They just respond and the man responded by giving the other man a very good clout to the jaw. It was a dilly and the man joined the woman in the street. They were so unconscious that they looked as if they had just been married and the crowd around them part of a crazy wedding reception.

Things were getting very far-out.

The two men continued crying. They had cried so much now that they were no longer human. It was not possible for that many tears to be contained in a human body. It was as if there were a spring of tears under their feet that bubbled up into their legs and fed their non-stop crying.

The mayor was totally berserk.

He was no longer shouting at the two men to stop crying or threatening them with the police.

He was shouting things that had no meaning like the license plate number of a car he had owned in 1947.

"AZ 1492!" he shouted.

"AZ 1492! AZ 1492! AZ 1492!" he kept shouting over and over again. Everytime he shouted his license plate number it seemed to provoke the crowd to a higher and higher state of agitation.

His license plate number was inciting a crowd to riot.

By this time it was noon and the high school was being let out for lunch. The high school was three blocks away on the Main Street of town and the students were now hurrying down the street toward the commotion.

"AZ 1492!" the mayor continued shouting. "AZ 1492!"

Half a dozen fights were now in progress in the crowd which had grown to several hundred with dozens more joining it every minute. The newcomers responded to the mayor's continued shouting of his license plate number by shoving other people and starting to shout things themselves.

"I hate you!" a seventy-one-year-old woman shouted at a total stranger, somebody she had never seen before in her life, and then she punched the person, who was an elderly man, right in the balls. He dropped like a stone to the street but was able to open the package he was carrying and take out a lemon cream pie that he had just purchased at the bakery and shove it into the old woman's knee.

"Pervert!" she shouted down at him as he lay there grinding the pie into her knee. Her knee looked odd covered with meringue and yellow filling that was now running down her leg and flowing into the top of her shoe.

Where were the police?

Why hadn't they arrived to stop this?

They had left the station which was five blocks away over ten minutes ago but they were nowhere in sight. Their presence at this time could have controlled the crowd and avoided a national tragedy.

Where were they?

Then three hundred high school kids arrived at the crowd and were drawn into it like a paper boat into a maelstrom.

Within a few moments there were acts of sexual intercourse going on in the street and a baby had been born. In a few days there would be pictures of the President of the United States holding that baby in his hands and declaring it a symbol of the future that must reunite the country.

The baby was a boy and its name was to be Ralph and its portrait was to be on a commemorative postage stamp. Unfortunately, at the present time things were not going well for the mother and her newly-born baby in this frenzied crowd of wild animals. The mother was screaming hysterically as she lay in the street. She begged the crowd not to step on her baby. The crowd responded to the plea by stepping on the mother instead of the baby.

The old man who had been punched in the balls by the old woman and then had revenged himself by shoving a lemon cream pie into her knee had long since been ground up into old man burger by thousands of rioting feet.

In a few days when the bodies would be sifted through for burial, the old man's body would be unrecognizable. When he went downtown to get the pie for his dinner, he didn't take any identification with him. He just took enough money to buy a pie. He was to be buried in a common grave with 225 other unfortunates who were not recognizable and did not have any identification on them.

In a few days there would also be photographs of the President standing beside their freshly-filled-in grave. Later on a very elegant monument would be put over the grave, and the monument and common grave would be reproduced on postcards that became quite popular.

The monument was to be a fine work of art commissioned by the Federal government and utilizing the talents of one of America's well-known sculptors.

But we're getting a little ahead of the story now.

Let us return to something basic.

Where were the police?

E_{ggs}

"I don't have any eggs," he said aloud to himself. He was still sitting on the couch. He was very surprised by this revelation. His scrambled egg house of cards came crashing down on him.

"There are no eggs in this house," he said.

There had never been an egg in the house. He liked to eat eggs but he didn't like to have them in the house. It was one of his "quirks." When he ate eggs it was almost always in a restaurant.

There was no logical reason why he did not have eggs in the house. It was just that he felt slightly uncomfortable when they were there. Also, he did not like to buy eggs. Something about the cartons put him off and he did not like the fact that they came in dozens.

When he ordered eggs in a restaurant there were just two of them. That was a controllable number of eggs to his thinking. Two eggs were not a commitment. They were just something to eat and enjoy.

A dozen eggs were a different matter.

They were *twelve* eggs.

That was just too many eggs to think about at one time.

After all, he had just so much time in life to think about eggs and twelve eggs occupied too much time, so he preferred not to have that many eggs in his house.

Once he went through the process of thinking about getting half-a-dozen eggs but that was still too many eggs. Six eggs automatically made him think of twelve eggs and he was right back where he started. Also, he didn't like the idea of a carton being cut in half. It seemed like an act of mutilation to him like somebody losing a leg.

He got up and went into the kitchen, anyway, looking for eggs, even though he knew that he didn't have any. He would use up a little time. After all, he had a broken heart and there was nothing better to do.

He opened up the refrigerator and looked inside.

"No eggs here," he said.

Train

As the riot was commencing on the Main Street of town, it is necessary to bring up a very important detail right now:

the train.

The railroad station was six blocks away from the riot and there was a train at the station. It was an eight-car freight train carrying property that belonged to the United States government, more specifically it belonged to the Army.

The train was carrying weapons and ammunition that was on its way to an Army post out in California.

That takes care of the important detail.

Sanctuary

Even though a riot was raging on the Main Street of town, the sombrero had not been disturbed. It had a small sanctuary in the center of the riot. The space was ten feet in diameter. It was as if there were an invisible fence around the small circle because people would not step into it. Life and death were now raging outside the circle but not a single person would venture into it.

There was no reason for them not to step into it.

They just didn't do it.

The circle was still occupied by the mayor who was still shouting his license plate number to the crowd who could no longer hear him. You could see his mouth moving but it was as if nothing were coming out. The roar of the crowd had turned the mayor into a mime.

The two men were still standing there crying.

That was their fate.

The people in the circle have now been taken care of.

Only the sombrero is left.

It was still lying in the street. No one had touched it. For no reason at all the crowd left it alone. Not a single person had stepped into the circle and tried to pick it up. The sombrero just lay there, unaltered or affected by the commotion going on about it.

Here are a couple of more interesting things about the sombrero:

1. It was not made in Mexico.

2. Yes, it did belong to somebody but they were very faraway.

Bacon

Even though he knew there were no eggs in the kitchen and there had never been any, he very carefully went through the ritual of looking for them.

"Not in the refrigerator, not in the pantry, not in the cupboard," he said to himself after he had checked them all out. He checked the refrigerator again to make sure.

Sometimes he talked to himself a lot and he was talking to himself about the absence of eggs in his apartment.

"Where are those eggs?" he said to himself. "They must be here somewhere," and all the time knowing that there were no eggs in the kitchen.

He was just starting to think about looking for them in other rooms, perhaps the bedroom, when a lightning bolt of despair suddenly fried his brain into thousands of pieces of dancing bacon. He remembered his love for the Japanese woman.

During the time that he was thinking about his hunger, he had forgotten about her. Then he thought about her and it was apocalyptic to his being. It just took one simple thought of her to purge hunger instantly from his body and return him to a condition of total despair.

He walked back into the front room and sat down on the couch. Halfway to the couch he had completely forgotten what he had been doing in the kitchen, that he had been searching for imaginary eggs. He would never remember it again nor any of the thoughts that he'd had about hamburgers or tuna fish sandwiches or the hunger itself that had briefly obsessed his life.

They were gone forever.

It was as if he had never been hungry that evening. When he would have breakfast the next morning at a restaurant, he would play half-heartedly with his food and finish only a small portion of it. Eating not to appease hunger but just to survive.

If you had told him that he had been very hungry last night and spent almost an hour thinking about food, he would have thought that you were nuts.

*S*hadow

Yukiko continued to sleep on, enjoying her dream of Kyoto and standing at her father's grave and somehow because the day was so beautiful, he wasn't dead. He wasn't alive but he wasn't dead either in her dream of Japanese autumn in a warm fine rain.

Her father was like the shadow purring of a cat.

He was in a purring space that was neither life nor death.

Yukiko wanted to purr, too, and answer him but she couldn't because she was alive, so she just enjoyed his presence.

As Yukiko lay there asleep and dreaming, her cat lay beside her asleep and purring.

Kaleidoscope

The American humorist sat on his couch suffering thoughts of her, trying to figure out how to win back her affections, wondering what had happened between them or just tumbling head-over-heels down into romantic oblivion where the image of a remembered kiss provokes bottomless despair and makes death seem like the right idea.

He experienced the basics of love ended.

Of course in his case these emotions were being played through a kaleidoscope of goofiness and insanity. But still he suffered genuinely and realistically as any other person. After all, he was still human. It was just that his mind translated this into a twelve-ring circus with most of the acts not worth watching a second time. After while non-stop brilliance has the same effect as non-stop boredom.

It was now 10:45 in the evening.

The night would be long for him.

He had been suffering from insomnia, so that when he tried to sleep it was like having a brain full of barbed wire.

Phantoms and fantasies of love raced back and forth across his mind, galloping as if on horses frenzied by snakes with no place else to go.

Then he thought about calling her on the telephone but he knew that she was in bed with somebody else and he would feel even worse when she answered the telephone.

He'd had enough suffering right now to last him forever with plenty left over for others if they didn't have enough and wanted to have some more.

He glanced over at the telephone sitting on a small table by a window that looked out over the late evening lights of San Francisco. To him the lights looked as if they had been painted on the window.

The sight of the telephone made him shudder. His neck and head trembled slightly. He was crazy but he wasn't stupid.

Dead

As the riot raged around the sombrero it remained safe in its little sanctuary in the middle of the crowd with its three companions: a crazy mayor still shouting his license plate number and two sobbing men who had been crying so long that they were like huge babies. They weren't even aware that they were crying any more. They didn't know where they were at or what they were doing.

Tears just flowed up through underground springs directly into the bottoms of their feet and went up through their bodies and came out their eyes . . . or so it seemed. Nothing else could explain where they were getting all those tears to cry with.

Those tears had to come from someplace, so it might as well be from hidden crying springs that came from deep in the earth and flowed great distances, originating at cemeteries and from cheap hotel rooms decorated in loneliness and despair.

Unfortunately, there is enough grief around to irrigate the Sahara.

What happened to the police?

Why weren't they there to stop the crowd from rioting, to nip this thing in the bud while it was still possible? If they had been there a national tragedy would have been avoided.

The police station was only a few blocks away. Somebody had called them and they had gotten into the two cars that were the police department in that small town, but they hadn't arrived yet. It was such a short distance for them to come.

Where were they?

That's simple enough.

Dead.

Temperature

When the sombrero fell out of the sky, it had a temperature of −24. A few moments ago with the riot raging around it, the temperature of the sombrero rose one degree to −23.

Interesting.

*P*ages

Yukiko turned like a fantastic page in her sleep and her hair turned also like a dark page. Her turning woke the cat up and the cat stopped purring. The cat thought about going back to sleep, then decided not to.

The cat lay there staring into the dark evening depths of the room. The cat was thirsty. Soon it would get out of bed and go into the kitchen and get some water from its dish by the refrigerator. It would probably have a little midnight snack, too. The cat would have five or six bits of dried cat food which it would eat very slowly: *crunch crunch crunch* like chewing soft diamonds in the dark.

Yukiko turned over again. She was becoming restless in her sleep. Her dream of Kyoto was falling apart at the edges. The dream depended on the purring of the cat for existence and now that the cat had stopped purring her dream was falling apart.

Her mind tried to create a synthetic purring but it was unable to. The dream needed the cat's purring to go on existing. Then the dream started to break up like a severe earthquake. Great chunks of it shook down. The warm autumn rain turned into ruins and the cemetery folded up like a disheveled card table and her feeling of peace and contentment turned into nothing.

The cat stood up in bed, stretched and then jumped down onto the floor. It walked very slowly to the kitchen, stopping on its way to stretch again.

By the time the cat reached the bowl of water beside the refrigerator in the kitchen, Kyoto was over.

Accident

Why were the police dead?

That's an easy one.

On their way to the riot in the town's two police cars, they had ingeniously managed a collision between the cars that had miraculously killed them all. It was the kind of accident that usually results in minor injuries with all parties concerned getting out of the cars and walking away, badly shaken of course but all in one piece.

That was not the case in this accident.

They had managed to kill themselves.

There were six police officers in the two cars and they were very dead. It was not a pretty sight. A closer viewing of details is not needed. Things should be left as they are. The town's police department had killed itself. It will be left there except to say that normally there would have been a huge crowd around such an accident. The streets would have been filled with curious people but because of the riot raging a few blocks away, there was nobody at the scene of the accident. The two cars were tangled together and filled with the bodies of dead policemen and not a single person was there. It was a very strange sight.

It looked unreal.

Nobody had even bothered to call the police station to tell the woman who worked there as a radio dispatcher what had happened.

After the first phone call telling about the riot, nobody else called in. They were all at the riot busy rioting, so she thought that everything was under control. She sat there in the police station doing her nails.

*J*uly

Thirty seconds later everything had turned around in his head and he decided to call her, anyway. There had to be an end to his suffering. It could not go on forever. By waking her up in the middle of the night and telling her that he loved her and would be on his way over to her apartment right away in a cab, that would solve it.

He got up from the couch and walked over to the telephone. He picked up the receiver and then he dialed the first digit of her number.

clickclickclickclickclickclickclick 7

Then he dialed the second digit.

clickclickclickclickclick 5

Love is a form of insanity.

He dialed the third digit.

clickclick 2

He had four more digits to go.

He was almost halfway there.

All he needed to do was to dial the remaining digits, wait while the telephone rang, then she would answer it and he would hear her voice and this is what she would have really said to him, being free of his fantasies of what she was doing and who she was and everything else that was ping-ponging around in his head.

Her voice would have been very sleepy.

She would have said, "Yes, who is it?"

He would have said, "It's me. I love you. I want to see you right now. Can I come over?"

"No, I don't want to see you," she would have said, and hung up.

That's what would have really happened.

She was tired of him.

She wanted to live her own life again.

She had no more time to give him.

She had given him all of her life that she could afford. She didn't have any more life to give him. She wanted to have some to live herself.

He started to dial the fourth digit but he never finished dialing it. He hung up the telephone. He walked back to the couch and sat down. He rubbed his eyes like an old man.

For about thirty seconds his mind had been totally blank which was very unusual for him because he almost always kept a Fourth of July parade going on in there.

"Jesus," he finally said aloud to himself. "I almost did it. I almost called her. I've got to get a grip on myself."

It was now 10:50 in the evening and he wasn't sleepy at all. He tried to think of something to do with the rest of the night.

The night turns long when love sours.

Replace

The cat drank some water in the dark kitchen and then started back down the hall to the bedroom where its Japanese mistress was sleeping.

Halfway down the hall, the cat remembered that it had forgotten to get something to eat. It always liked to snack on a few chunks of dry cat food in the night after it had a little water to drink.

The cat walked back to the kitchen.

It had another drink of water and then it started eating some cat food while the Japanese woman lay sleeping.

Yukiko was resting in that space between dreams.

Kyoto was gone.

Soon something else would replace it.

Yukiko's mouth was slightly open and her breathing passed softly through it.

She liked to dream because she seldom ever had any

nightmares. Her dreams were a pleasant diversion. She'd never had a night's insomnia in her life because she always looked forward to falling asleep, so that she could dream.

Though filled with grief, she fell asleep instantly the night of her father's suicide years ago in Seattle and even had good dreams that night. She dreamt that her father was not dead, that he would wake her for school in the morning like he always did.

Cobwebs

The American humorist had to do something with the night that was growing long about him. He had no interest in sleep. He just couldn't sit there alone in his apartment until it was day. He didn't want to do that.

Then he thought of something.

He walked over to the telephone and dialed a number.

It was not the Japanese woman's number.

The number belonged to an airline stewardess that he had dated on and off for years. She often stayed up late if she was in town. She was one of those women who didn't like to go out very much but instead liked to futz around her apartment, doing little things, listening to the phonograph or knitting or any of a hundred small nocturnal tasks that you can do in your apartment by yourself late at night.

Maybe it was the flying around all over the country every few days that made her want to stay home at night.

She was sitting on the rug reading a copy of *Cosmopolitan* when the telephone rang.

She knew there was only one person in the world who would call her that late at night. She put the magazine down and crawled across the floor to the telephone. She reached up on a table and brought the telephone down to the floor.

"Hello, night owl," she said cheerfully.

She was always cheerful.

"What are you doing?" he said.

"Nothing," she said. "Just sitting here reading all about how attractive adultery can be. You haven't gotten married recently, have you?"

"No," he said. "Why should I get married?"

"Because that would make you more attractive to a lonely little stewardess who wants to be a Cosmogirl. This month we're only supposed to go to bed with married men."

He didn't know what she was talking about. He didn't even think it was funny but it's already been mentioned before that he had no sense of humor.

There was a big smile on her face as she held the telephone to her ear. She knew that he could not see any humor in what she'd just said.

She tried hard not to laugh.

She always thought that it was very ironic and amusing that he very seldom thought that anything was funny.

"What are you doing?" he repeated.

"Nothing," she said. "Just sitting here reading all about how attractive adultery can be. You haven't gotten married recently, have you?"

There was a pause at his end of the telephone.

She could tell that he was confused.

"Why don't you come over?" she said.

"OK," he said. "But first, what did you just say?"

"I said why don't you come over," she said. "I'm not doing anything. I'd like to see you. Bring something to drink. I'd like some wine. Got any wine over there?"

"Yeah, I've got some wine."

"Bring it over. We'll have a drink together and talk about old times or maybe start some new ones."

"I'll be there in twenty minutes," he said.

"Make it nineteen," she said.

"OK," he said. "I'll be there as soon as I can. Is white all right?"

"Fine," she said.

They hung up.

She had a big smile on her face.

She crawled back over to her *Cosmopolitan* and resumed the article about adultery. She enjoyed reading the article because it made absolutely no sense at all.

She was very cheerful.

She came from Texas.

Her father was the fire chief in a small town that once went three years without having a fire.

There was an article about him in *Life* magazine with a photograph of him standing beside his fire engine. The fire engine was covered with fake cobwebs.

He had a big smile on his face.

He was cheerful, too.

It ran in the family.

Barbell

The temperature of the sombrero was now
−23.

The hat had gone up one degree as the crowd continued to riot. Most of the people in the crowd did not know why they were rioting. When they had arrived on the scene there was already a riot going on, so they just joined in: yelling punching screaming smashing kicking for no reason except the fact that other people were doing it and they looked as if they were having a lot of fun.

Most of the people in the crowd did not know that there was a sombrero in a circle at the center of the riot and of course they had no way of knowing that the temperature of the sombrero had originally been 24 degrees below zero and that it was now rising.

The sombrero went up another degree to −22 and a few

minutes later it was at −21. It was a steady and rapid rise now. Then it was −20 and still rising.

−19 and still rising
−18 and still rising
−17 and still rising
−16 and still rising
−15 and still rising
−14 and still rising
−13 and still rising

As the temperature of the sombrero rose higher and higher the intensity of the riot increased.

People were really bashing each other now.

A ten-year-old boy poked a stick into the eye of an old woman.

−12 and still rising

The two crying men had cried so long and hard now that they could barely stand up.

−11 and still rising

"AZ 1492!" the mayor shouted.

−10 and still rising

A cheerleader-type high school girl split the lip of the town banker. He responded to this by ripping the girl's blouse off and punching her in the breast. Then he threw her onto the ground, trying to get her pants off and unzip his fly with just about the same motion.

He didn't get very far with this because (−9 and still rising) a beauty shop operator jumped right in the middle of his back with her high heels.

She didn't get to enjoy the effect of this for very long because a few seconds later she was rendered unconscious with an alarm clock.

A man had been on his way to the town fixit shop to have his clock repaired when he joined in the riot, so he just hit the woman over the head with it. She dropped in her tracks which happened to be grinding her heels into the banker's back like a barbell.

—8 and still rising

In a few hours they would be using the same energy that they attacked each other with against the National Guard and US paratroopers.

These were a fierce people.

—7 and still rising

The sombrero was getting hotter.

Bridge

He of course did not visit the cheerful and intelligent stewardess who would have been able to take his mind off his broken heart. That would have been too easy. No, he didn't want to do anything like that. It would have compromised his basic approach to life which was to have it as confusing, labyrinth-laden and fucked up as possible.

She was just finishing the article on adultery in *Cosmopolitan* when he called her back.

"What's up?" she said, knowing it was him when she picked up the receiver. "You're not coming."

That surprised him.

"How did you know?"

"I've known you for five years," she said. "That's a lot of water under the bridge."

She was smiling when she said it.

She was always cheerful.

Her sunny side was always up.

There was a pause on the other end of the line.

"What water?" he said.

"Just water, dear," she said, still smiling. She could see his mind wrestling with that one. It was simply amazing. *Boy, would his readers be surprised if they ever met him,* she thought.

"How about lunch next week?" he said.

"Fine," she said. "What day?"

"Maybe Wednesday. I'll call you on Monday to firm it up."

"That would be great," she said, knowing that he wouldn't call her on Monday and they wouldn't have lunch on Wednesday and she probably wouldn't hear from him for months until one night just like a little while ago, he would call her and ask her if he could come over and he would either come over or not come over.

There was no way of knowing.

He was really quite mad but she liked him because he unknowingly amused her and he was good in bed. He wasn't as good in bed as he thought he was but he was OK.

She had no big hopes for him.

She couldn't resist playing around with his mind a little before he hung up.

"Do you know where I'd like to eat?" she said.

"Where?" he said.

"At the little Italian restaurant we used to eat at a couple of years ago. Remember the one on Columbus Avenue? With the fat waitress?"

"Yes," he said, not remembering it at all.

"I'd like to eat there."

"Sure," he said. "That would be fun. We'll eat there. I'll call you on Monday."

"Great," she said. "I can hardly wait."
He never called.
They didn't have lunch.

Cape Kennedy

          −6 and still rising
     −5 and still rising
     −4 and still rising
     −3 and still rising

H*air*

After he hung up, he wondered why he had called her in the first place. He liked her but he didn't want to see her right now. Maybe later but not now.

"I wonder what in the hell I was thinking about?" he said aloud to himself. "I wonder if I'm losing my mind?"

That was like a duck wondering why it flies south in the autumn or an old camel noticing one day that he has a hump on his back.

He went into the bathroom to get a glass of water and found a long black hair in the sink. When he saw the hair his heart sank like a rock. He carefully picked it up and looked at it. He looked at the hair very slowly. It was hard for him to believe that the hair was in his hand.

After he finished examining it, he took the hair back into the living room with him and he sat down on the couch and continued looking at the hair.

He turned it over very slowly in his hand and then he rubbed it together between his fingers. The hair had totally captured his concentration.

He was so fascinated by the long single strand of black hair that he did not overflow his mind with fantasies about it, turning it into a hundred varieties of his imagination.

He just sat there staring at it.

Japanese hair.

E_{ars}

—2 and still rising

—1 and still rising

—0 blast off! We have a go! We have a go here!

A state police car came around a corner and stopped at the edge of the riot. The police car had accidentally stumbled upon the riot. They had no idea what they would see when they came around the corner. They had not received a call about the riot over their radio. They were just driving through town on their way north a few miles where on certain days they liked to set up a speed trap.

"What in the hell!" one of the state troopers said to his partner. "Get on the radio!" was the second thing he said. Then he said, "Where are the fucking police in this town?" The fourth thing he said was, "We're going to need some help and pronto!"

His partner finally said his first thing. He said, "Shit! I

wanted to get home to my kid's birthday party this afternoon. What are these fuckers doing?"

The presence of the police car was barely noticed by the crowd until the talkative policeman got out of the car, while the other one was radioing for all the help they could get, and discharged his pistol in the air.

The police officer did a very bad job of firing his gun in the air. It bore no resemblance to things like that you see on television or in the movies because he blew the ear off an old dignified woman. He blew it right off her head spraying blood on all the people around her.

That was the last thing in the world that was needed to calm down this group of already rioting citizens.

They responded to the town librarian having her ear blown off by attacking the policeman and literally tearing him to bits. They also dragged his partner out of the police car and gave him a good killing, too, but not before he shot three of them, including the town librarian. It was the second time that she had been shot in five minutes.

The bullet took off her other ear.

The town now possessed an earless librarian.

A lot of towns won't stand for things like that and this was one of those towns. After killing the two police officers, they took their very ragged-looking bodies and threw them on the now burning car.

The crowd had stopped fighting each other by now and had united in anger against these outsiders coming in and shooting the ears off their librarian.

They were all brothers and sisters now.

Black flames tornadoed themselves up into the clean blue sky. The smell of burning police cars mingled with the smell of burning policemen.

The crowd cheered lustily.

They had tasted blood.

And they were in a mood for tasting more.

It was then that two more state police cars drove up on the scene and within a few minutes a gun battle had broken out between the police and the crowd.

The crowd was using the weapons of the two dead officers.

The police blasted into the crowd with their shotguns trying to break them up. The crowd fired back and rushed as one person the state police and human-waved over them.

The street was littered with the wounded and dying.

Then there were two more burning police cars pyring their former masters who burned on top of them.

Dozens of the crowd had by now rushed to their nearby homes to get guns. The crowd was arming itself against the outside world that had descended upon them to shoot the ears off their librarian.

They would not stand idly by and be slaughtered.

"Death to all outsiders!" somebody yelled.

"Death! Death! Death!" the crowd chanted.

These people were in a bad mood.

A couple of more state police cars showed up but they were immediately driven off by a heavy concentration of gunfire from the townspeople.

The state police couldn't figure out what in the hell had come over this town. It had always been a typical, friendly place to live. It was as if the town had suddenly become possessed.

More state police cars showed up and they, too, were driven off, some of them getting killed and in turn killing some townspeople.

The police decided not to attempt to shoot their way into town but to stay on the outskirts and increase their numbers until they had a sufficient force to mount an assault on the town, but before they attacked they would try to talk the people into laying down their arms and surrendering peacefully.

They thought they would be able to talk some sense to the town.

The governor had already been informed of the situation and was on his way in a helicopter. The police departments of neighboring towns were also contributing men to the possible assault force and the pièce de résistance was on its way. That was an armored car that had been borrowed from the National Guard. It had two mounted .50 calibre machine guns that should be able to talk sense to any crowd of rioting citizens.

The captain in charge of the state police told the governor that everything would be under control within a couple of hours.

They were talking on the telephone.

This was just before both of them got into separate helicopters and flew directly to the scene.

"What in the hell's going on down there?" the governor said.

"I don't know," the captain said. "But we'll have it under control shortly."

Then the governor told the captain that he was going down there to have a look at the scene himself. The governor did not want anything like the Attica business going on in his state which was quite liberal. He thought that Rockefeller should have gone to Attica and stopped it. He couldn't afford any big political mistakes right now because he was up for re-election in the autumn. He was going for his second term and he didn't want anything to fuck it up.

When a town of 11,000 people suddenly goes crazy and

126

starts killing police officers that was a potentially very explosive political situation and he wanted it totally under control.

The captain didn't want the governor to go down there because he thought that it reflected on his ability to handle the situation and he was a very proud man. He had been in charge of the state police for nine years and had worked his way up through the ranks.

He had been a member of the state police for thirty-two years.

"I'll be down there in about forty minutes," the governor said after he had told the captain that he was going down there.

"There's no need for you to go down there," the captain said. "This thing will be over in just a few hours. As soon as I get down there I'll take care of it and then I'll come up to the capital and give you a firsthand report."

"This is *my* state," the governor said. "I'll be down there in forty minutes. I don't want another Attica down there."

"Attica?" the captain said.

"Yes, Attica!" the governor shouted.

"Oh, Attica," the captain said. He wondered what in the hell the governor was talking about. He looked at his watch to see if it was after lunch. The governor sometimes had a couple of stiff belts during lunch.

There was a little joke in the state about not having any serious business with the governor until around three in the afternoon. That's when he sobered up.

The captain imagined the smell of whiskey coming out of the telephone receiver. He shuddered. He had once been a drinking man and had to give it up if he wanted to advance in the state police, so he gave up drinking. It had been a very hard thing for him to do.

127

He really liked to drink whiskey, and there he was with a slightly drunk governor on the other end of the line who wanted to go down there and get into what was police business and now he'd have to worry about the governor catching a bullet or messing up his strategy for handling the rioters.

"I'll see you down there," the governor said, waiting for the response that would show who was boss.

"Yes, sir," the captain said.

Drowning

He was still sitting there on the couch staring at the strand of long black hair in his hand. His imagination remained immobile. Not even so much as a mouse ran across it. His whole life was now just Japanese hair. He had no other perception of the world and it was as if nothing else had ever happened to him except Japanese hair.

He turned the strand of hair over in his fingers and lost control of it and it fell away, disappearing on the floor. Panicstricken he fell on his knees, looking desperately for it, but it did not allow itself to be found easily.

He was turning into a madman scrambling around on the floor, looking for the strand of Japanese hair.

He was on the edge of screaming as he looked for the hair. He thought that he would go mad if he didn't find that strand of hair right now.

Then his whole life flashed in front of him like a drowning man, all for the loss of Japanese hair.

Trainmaster

The trainmaster, a kindly old gentleman, came down from the station to see what was happening when he heard all the shooting and stuff going on downtown and what had happened was that his wife had had her ears blown off and then to make matters worse she had also been shot dead.

His wife was of course the town librarian.

She had caught some more lead when the second group of state policemen had arrived on the scene and engaged the crowd in a gun battle.

The trainmaster responded to the occurrence of having a dead earless wife by informing the crowd about the train full of weapons and ammunition waiting at the depot.

He didn't know what had occurred to cause all the trouble including the death of his wife, but he was ready to fight, anyway. He wanted revenge at any cost and he wasn't going to quibble about details of right or wrong.

He stood there for a moment staring at his dead no-eared wife and then he yelled, "Guns for killing!"

This was his opening statement to inform the crowd of the arsenal that was only a few blocks away, waiting for their use.

"Guns for killing!" he repeated.

Twenty minutes later the crowd was armed to the teeth with the finest collection of hardware outside of Indo-China during the great Vietnam War days.

The crowd had taken a liking to his first words of weapon introduction and now they were all shouting, "Guns for killing! Guns for killing!"

And they waved their guns in the air.

"Guns for killing!"

And some of them discharged their weapons in the air.

"Guns for killing!"

Mean folks . . .

M-16

Somehow the mayor and his cousin and the unemployed man ended up heavily armed, too. They all had M-16s and lots of grenades.

The mayor was still shouting out his license plate number, "AZ 1492!"

His senses were totally shattered, but somebody gave him a gun, some ammunition and a lot of grenades, anyway. Nobody cared. Everybody was crazy.

His cousin and the unemployed man were still crying, but now they were clutching rifles to their chests that heaved in sobbing.

When they were given guns, the logic was that crying people can shoot, too.

Every trigger finger counts.

The mayor and the two men barely knew that they were armed.

They held their rifles awkwardly like sticks.

"AZ 1492!" the mayor shouted.

"No," a young Vietnam combat veteran said. "That's an M-16. Not as good as an AK-47 but it will do the job."

Lemonade

While he was driven to desperation over one
strand of Japanese hair, an entire head of it, long and beautiful and so very black, lay sleeping in the Richmond District of San Francisco.

Thank heaven he did not have this thought.

He would have turned it into a razor sharp obsession. It
would have heightened his feeling of despair over the
ending of his affair with the Japanese woman.

*Here I am changed into a madman looking for a single
strand of Japanese hair when for two years I had access to a
whole head of it.*

That would have made him feel horrible.

The bottom would have fallen out of the bottom of his
life.

Yes, it was very good that he did not have that thought as

he scrambled around on the floor with his whole life flashing in front of him.

He was drowning in a strand of Japanese hair.

That strand of lost hair was the same as falling overboard in the middle of the Pacific Ocean. He struggled for breath while his life like an overexposed home movie flashed from scene to scene in the front room of his mind with all of his relatives and friends and lovers watching it on a hot summer evening with glasses of ice-cold lemonade in their hands, interested when they were on the screen and bored when they weren't, except for his lovers who were all interested in whom he was going to bed with.

There was only one person missing from the movie.

And she was asleep sixteen blocks away.

She had enough long black hair, Japanese hair, to keep on drowning him forever.

N_{ose}

The sombrero was alone in the center of the street: its only company burning police cars and a bunch of dead bodies.

There were lots of people coming and going with guns but nobody paid any attention to the sombrero. The temperature of the sombrero remained at zero. It's interesting that nobody noticed the sombrero. It's only logical with so many people milling around in the street that somebody would have noticed the sombrero and put it on their head or at least attempted to until they noticed that the sombrero was ice-cold.

But that was not the case.

Everybody passed by the sombrero as if it were invisible. The sombrero of course was not invisible. It was as plain as the nose on your face. You couldn't miss it. The sombrero was in plain sight for the whole world to see.

Then suddenly an old man looked straight at the sombrero and headed toward it, but when he was about five feet away from the sombrero, he stopped and looked straight down.

He stood there and stared at a small blown-off part of a human being. That was what he was heading for in the first place. It wasn't the sombrero at all. It was just that the sombrero was in a direct visual line with the piece of human.

The old man had never seen a chunk of person before without the rest of the person attached.

He was fascinated.

Saucers

State police and nearby law enforcement officers who had set up positions outside of town waited for the captain in charge of the state police to arrive and personally direct operations to put down what had started off with a sombrero falling out of the sky and now had progressed into an armed rebellion.

From time to time heavy gunfire left the town in search of the lawmen who were entrenched outside of the city limits, waiting for the captain to arrive, so that they could get on with putting down the rebellion.

The officers crouching down in ditches tried to figure out what had happened to the town to change its people into blood-thirsty rebels, but they couldn't come up with a single answer.

They had no way of knowing about the sombrero and what happened after it fell out of the sky.

"What in the hell's going on in there?" a state police sergeant said to a deputy sheriff from the next town.

"I don't know," the deputy said. "They've all gone Goddamn fucking crazy. I've never seen anything like this before. I sure hope it ain't flying saucers."

"Flying saucers?" the sergeant said.

"Yeah, you know flying saucers," the deputy sheriff said. "Creatures from outerspace taking over people's minds. Flying saucers," he repeated. "Flying saucers. From Mars."

The deputy sheriff's eyes were very bright.

The sergeant excused himself and went over to talk to another state policeman. The sergeant had a low tolerance for nuts even if they were fellow lawmen. He'd had an aunt who was crazy and he spent his whole childhood living in the same house with her. His family wouldn't send her off to the insane asylum. His father always said, "No relative of ours is going to the nuthouse," so the aunt lived with them and was quite mad.

They always had to lock her up in her room during Christmas because for some reason Christmas seemed to set her off, so every Christmas of his childhood was spent listening to his mad aunt screaming and banging on the door to her room.

The deputy sheriff had told the last person in the world that he should have told about his flying saucer theory.

The sergeant looked over at the deputy sheriff and shuddered.

Violin

After having quenched its thirst and enjoyed a little midnight snack, the cat returned to the side of its sleeping mistress.

The cat jumped into bed.

The cat lay down beside her.

The cat did a moment's methodical cleaning of its front paws.

The cat used its tongue like a violin bow on a slow piece of music.

The cat was purring as it licked itself.

When the cat started purring Yukiko started dreaming again but this time she dreamt of America. She was dreaming of Seattle.

And again: Her father was an unseen character in the dream. He was there in essence but did not possess a physical representation. He was everything in the dream that you couldn't see.

And again: It was not an unpleasant dream.

And it was raining in the dream and she was walking in the rain but it was a spring rain instead of an autumn rain and it was Seattle instead of Kyoto and she was on her way to visit a girlfriend instead of her father's grave.

The cat stopped cleaning itself and fell asleep but it did not stop purring. It continued to purr in its sleep and as it purred the Japanese woman dreamt on.

The cat's purring was the motor that ran the Japanese woman's dreaming.

Mailer

Meanwhile, news of the town's rebellion was being broadcast over the radio and on special television announcements. Concerned folks who had relatives or friends there were driving to the town and trying to get in, but the police had put up roadblocks and were turning people back.

There were of course sensation seekers who were looking only for excitement that were also being turned around at the roadblocks and sent back.

The thing was growing in size.

Already a garbled, almost incoherent, version of what was happening in the town was going out over the wire services. The town was about an hour away from a full-scale media invasion. The calm before the storm, as they say.

In a few hours there would be media command posts sending out every true and false detail to a news-hungry world that would be totally captivated by a small town in the Southwest whose entire populace had gone mad and taken on the military might of the United States.

Norman Mailer's arrival was sixteen hours away.

He would look tired when he got off the airplane at a nearby town.

It had been a long hard flight.

"What's going on here?" would be his first words when he touched ground.

There would be a couple of reporters waiting to interview him. They were nervous because they were young and liked Mailer a great deal.

Then Mailer would look at them suspiciously. He wondered why they were interviewing him instead of being at the town writing about what was going on there.

"Are you Norman Mailer?" one of the reporters said nervously, even though he knew that it was Norman Mailer. He stood there with a pad and pencil in his hands waiting for Norman Mailer to say that he was Norman Mailer, so that he could write it down.

"Got to get to work," Mailer said and walked over to a waiting car that was to take him to the town.

"Was that Norman Mailer?" the young reporter would say to his colleague. Even his colleague was put off by that and looked away in embarrassment.

"That was Norman Mailer," the young reporter would say to himself now because Norman Mailer was gone and his colleague was looking away.

"Norman Mailer," the young reporter wrote down on his pad. That's all he wrote.

Norman Mailer.

Telephones

Let us set the clock back because we are sixteen hours ahead of the story. We will return to telephones ringing in the town as news of the rebellion was being broadcast over the radio and television, and people started calling friends and loved ones in the town, wanting to know what was happening.

Hundreds of calls were being made but nobody was answering the telephone. There were telephones ringing everywhere in town but the townspeople just ignored them, lost as they were in riot madness, arming themselves and preparing to take on the military might of the United States.

The telephones in town just rang and rang and rang.

It was eerie.

They rang on and on and on.

Nobody was answering the telephone in an entire town.

All the people heard at the other end of the line was unrequited ringing.

It was as if the town had left this century.

Its isolation was that complete.

Logic

Just when the American humorist's mind was about to sink to the bottom of the ocean, logic like a life-jacket was thrown to him and he stopped drowning.

His mind was suddenly very clear and coherent.

He got up off the floor and went into the kitchen.

He opened a drawer and took out a flashlight.

Then he went into the room where he did his writing and got a magnifying glass.

Yes, logic now ruled his existence.

He very carefully got down on his knees again and held the magnifying glass to the floor and shined the flashlight through it.

He slowly analyzed the floor inch by inch.

He was like a child astronomer scanning the skies with a Sears and Roebuck telescope looking for a new comet that would be given his name because it accidentally crossed his telescope and nobody had ever seen it before or bothered to mention it, if they had seen it, thinking that somebody else had already discovered it.

The only difference between him and the astronomer was that instead of looking for fame in the sky, he was looking for a Japanese hair on the floor but a moment later he had the same feeling of discovery when he saw the hair lying there. It was so simple and alone in its existence. He wondered why he hadn't seen it before because it was lying so obviously in front of him.

Life is a mystery, he thought as he very carefully and happily picked up the hair. He picked it up in such a way that it would be very difficult for him to drop.

In other words: He had a good grip on a single strand of Japanese hair.

P_{ilot}

Meanwhile back in the waste paper basket—

two helicopters, one containing the captain in charge of the state police and the other the governor of the state, were on their way to the small town where hell reigned.

The governor was sobering up very fast.

I'm not going to let this thing turn into another Attica, he thought to himself.

He turned to one of his aides in the helicopter and asked him how long it would be before they were there.

The aide asked the pilot.

The pilot said, "What?"

He was shocked.

"How long will it be before we're there?" the aide repeated, wondering what was happening with the pilot.

"Oh, I thought you said something else," the pilot said.

"What did you think I said?" the aide said.

"Nothing. I just thought you said something else," the pilot said. Under no condition was he going to tell the governor's aide what he thought the aide said. They would take away his pilot's license. He didn't want that to happen, so he pretended stupidity. Better to be thought stupid than crazy.

"When in the fuck are we going to be there!" the governor shouted to his aide, though it would have been just as easy for the governor to ask the pilot himself because he was sitting next to the pilot and the aide was in a seat behind the pilot.

The pilot started to turn to the governor and tell him but he caught himself just before he did it and turned his head slightly back to the aide behind him and said, "About fifteen minutes."

"Fifteen minutes," the aide said to the governor.

"Fifteen minutes," the governor repeated, still thinking about Attica.

Waitress

The captain wasn't very happy in his helicopter. He had always liked the previous governor of the state and got along very well with him.

He did not care for the current governor and their relationship at best had always been strained.

The captain did not care for the governor's lunchtime drinking and also the governor was seeing a cocktail waitress in the capital, even though he was already married and had three children.

The governor was very careful to conceal his relationship with the waitress but still a lot of people who shouldn't have known about it, knew about it.

As the helicopter sped along through the sky, taking the captain closer and closer to a town that had gone crazy, the captain was worrying more and more about the governor showing up there.

The captain thought that it was a grandstand play and no good was going to come from it, none at all.

Why couldn't this fucking clown just stay up in the capital and get drunk and screw his cocktail waitress and leave police business to the police?

Spring

It was a very beautiful spring day in Seattle in Yukiko's dream. There were flowers blooming out an emerging unbelievable intensity of lush greenness as she walked along in her dream.

She was halfway to her friend's house.

She was going to see her best friend: a Caucasian girl that she still corresponded with and saw once a year either in Seattle or in San Francisco.

In the dream Yukiko was fifteen years old.

The rain fell steadily. It was a slightly cold rain but she was wearing clothes that protected her from it and she felt no discomfort. Though the rain was cold, she was warm and dry.

She carried an umbrella.

It was an umbrella that her father had gotten for her in Japan, so she carried it lovingly.

As was mentioned in a previous chapter, her father was an essence in the dream. He did not have a physical body. He was everything that you couldn't see in the dream. He hadn't killed himself yet, so his existence in the dream was that of being alive.

That's all.

He was alive in the dream.

His being alive was everything that you couldn't see in her dream.

*L*ove

The word Attica hung like a comic strip balloon in the governor's mind as he looked out the window of the helicopter and saw another helicopter.

"There's the captain," his aide said, noticing the helicopter, too.

"Yeah, that's the captain," the governor said in a voice that showed that he had no use for the captain. There was no love lost between them.

The town was coming into view in front of them.

The two helicopters were just a few moments away.

The captain looked over at the governor's helicopter. They were only about a quarter of a mile apart. The captain was not pleased by the sight of the governor's helicopter.

"Shit," he said.

The captain then got on the helicopter radio and contacted a state police unit on the ground near the town. "What's happening down there?" he said.

"These people have all gone crazy," was the response.

"Well, I'll take care of that," the captain said.

He was a very efficient lawman. Also, he was slightly arrogant. The arrogance had been one of the aftereffects of his giving up drinking.

The captain suddenly noticed that the helicopters had gotten a lot closer to each other. They were only about a hundred yards apart.

"We're not too close, are we?" he said to the pilot, gesturing toward the governor's helicopter nearby in the sky.

"Oh, no. Everything's OK," the pilot said.

At that very instant the governor's pilot was reassuring the aide that they weren't too close.

"Don't worry," he said to the aide. "This is precious cargo."

What if this turns out to be another Attica? the governor thought to himself. *That could be my goose. I've got all that money behind me for re-election and I don't want to blow it.*

Clothes

The American humorist felt very good as he sat down on the couch with the hair in his hand. He had a good grip on it. He wouldn't lose it again. He sat there resting for a few moments. He had really gone through a lot of strenuous activity looking for the hair.

But that was the past now.

The hair was no longer lost.

He had found it and he felt good.

He looked at it in his hand.

Then his imagination started up.

The hair became a bridge between him and his lost Japanese lady. He thought about the first time he had touched her hair. It was that evening that he had met her at the bar and she had gone back to his apartment with him.

She had taken her clothes off before he did and was in bed waiting for him, watching him finish undressing.

Then he got into bed with her.

He felt as if he had brushed up against electricity as their bodies touched under the covers for the first time. A feeling of abstraction instantly replaced the electrical feeling of touching her.

Then he felt slightly dizzy.

I'm in bed with a Japanese woman, he thought.

It was suddenly very unreal to him even though he could feel her body touching him. Her skin was the same as any other woman's but he had never felt any skin quite like it before.

She reached over and put her hand gently on his stomach and he automatically reached over and cupped her head in his hand and turned his body into her and drew her mouth to his and kissed her softly upon the lips.

That was the first time he had touched her hair.

He did it very confidently in one graceful motion. It excited her. She did not know that he would be like this in bed. He spent the next two hours making love to her. It was very skillfully done but without being mechanical.

She was very pleased and impressed and had two fine orgasms. Normally, she only had one orgasm and she was surprised when she had the second one. Whenever she did have a second orgasm, it was usually a very small one but her second orgasm with him was as large as the first one which had her almost screaming.

He was surprised that she made so much noise during their love-making. He thought that she would be very quiet during sex because she was so quiet, anyway.

Her moaning turned him on. It was so incongruous that he found it very exciting.

While they made love he was constantly cradling and

stroking her hair and he felt that her hair was caressing him back.

When they were finally through with their love-making and lying silently beside each other, touching abstractly because passion had taken away all the reality from their bodies, he felt as if he had been to a place that he had never been before and the only passport there was a Japanese woman who moaned and sighed and moaned again until she was almost screaming as he made love to her.

That was the first time he touched her hair.

Once he bit her very gently but just enough for her to make a noise like two branches of a cherry tree rubbing together at night in a spring storm with a heavy warm wind blowing all around.

Two years later, he sat there holding a strand of her hair, staring at it like a madman.

Silence

A couple of state policemen on the ground were watching the approaching helicopters.

"Those helicopters sure are close together," one of them said.

"That's right," the other one said. He was a big strong brave loyal officer but he was not known for his thinking powers. He usually just went along with whatever anybody else was saying.

"It makes me a little nervous," the first officer said. "That's our captain and the governor up there. Why in the hell are they so close together? I don't like it."

The not-so-bright officer just shook his head. He couldn't find any words in his head to agree with what had just been said, so he just shook his head.

Besides, that was just as good as saying anything, anyway. He sometimes wondered why people talked at all. If people didn't talk then he wouldn't be nervous trying to figure out things to answer them with.

Talking was a waste of time was his theory.

Three or four times he had arrested people without saying a single word to them.

"What did I do, officer?"

Silence.

"I demand my rights!"

More silence.

"You can't handcuff me without telling me what I did. My cousin's a lawyer!"

Deeper silence.

"Jesus Christ! Ouch! I can't believe this. It must be a dream. Things like this don't happen in real life. Ouch! Not so tight!"

Speaking to just plain blue silence:

"Maybe I'll wake up."

D_{oll}

Yukiko could see cars and trees and flowers and houses and lawns and fences and people that she did not recognize going about their activities on a rainy day in a dream and everything that she could not see was her father still alive.

He had not killed himself and there was no stepfather calling her "China Doll."

Yukiko looked forward to seeing her friend.

She enjoyed the steady falling of the rain.

She could feel her father all around her.

He was everything that she couldn't see.

She carried her umbrella proudly like a magic wand.

A_{dios}

The midair collision was spectacular.
The helicopters looked like two, tall awkward people get-ting tangled up together in a revolving door during an earth-quake.
Then the bottom dropped out.
Good-bye, Captain.
Adios, Governor.

$$C R A S H !$$

so long

President

The hostilities between the town and the rest of the world escalated like a crown fire or a head-on automobile accident at ninety miles an hour or a tornado hitting a jellybean factory on Halloween.

It was awful.

There was a tremendous confusion among the lawmen laying siege to the town after the state police captain and the governor were killed.

In their disorder they launched an all-out attack on the town and got their asses shot off. There was just too much firepower in the town due to the emotional confiscation of the munitions train.

The retreating lawmen were stunned by the fury of the defenders and their awesome firepower.

A lot of them were killed or wounded.

Actually, they were practically wiped out.

ImMEDIAtely their attack and subsequent rout were referred to as a massacre but that was only going to last a few days before the President of the United States brought an abrupt halt to it with his battlefield speech of reconciliation and binding the nation's wounds.

The mayor killed one sheriff and wounded a deputy in the attack.

His cousin and the unemployed man, still weeping, managed only to shoot each other. It was an accident, but still they were dead.

What can you say?

Rest in Peace.

Emergency

Four hours later the National Guard was battling the town using tanks, armored cars and artillery. The townspeople fought back with the fury of trapped animals, thousands of them armed with automatic weapons.

The National Guard in the state had been allowed to really go down hill after the war in Vietnam ended. Their meetings and training had become very sloppy. Their attitude was bad, too. It was a kind of what-the-fuck attitude which was not the mental state to be in when suddenly confronted with a heavily-armed berserk town.

The National Guard suffered heavy casualties in a very short period of time. The whole state was in chaos with the governor dead and the captain of the state police dead and a lot of law enforcement officers suddenly dead and the National Guard undergoing a thorough routing.

Something had to be done. A senator from the state made an emergency telephone call to the President.

The President listened quietly for ten minutes and then said, "I'll authorize Federal troops to go to the scene. We'll get this under control for you. You have no idea how or why this got started?"

"No," the senator said. "We've got some theories but nothing concrete yet. We're working on it."

The senator of course had no theories.

There was an airplane waiting at the airport in Washington to take him immediately to the scene. He hadn't the slightest idea what the fuck was up. All he knew was that the governor was dead, hundreds of lawmen and National Guardsmen had been killed and that a whole town had gone crazy for no apparent reason.

"Thank you for the troops, Mr. President."

"Any time."

Loudspeakers

Even after Paratroopers and Special Forces and Rangers and Regular Army troops had arrived on the scene, the town held out for three days of bloody fighting.

During one lull in the battle a radio network hooked up to the White House broadcast a plea from the President to the town pleading with them to surrender.

The Army Corps of Engineers surrounded the town with loudspeakers that carried the President's message to the townspeople.

United States warplanes that had previously been bombing and strafing the town flew over dropping thousands of hastily printed leaflets that promised safe conduct to all who surrendered and a willingness to listen to any grievances the people had.

The only contact the people in the town had had so far with the outside world was gunfire.

They had issued no proclamations or demands.

They had no cause.

All they wanted was blood.

And blood was what they got.

Though they had inflicted heavy casualties against three separate groups of attackers, they had themselves taken a lot of casualties. Especially after the artillery and bombings started, but they were very brave and fought on against what were now overwhelming odds.

These townspeople had true grit.

Their mayor had become quite a hero to the people. He had taken over military leadership of them and directed them brilliantly in their game but losing battle.

Only from time to time now did the mayor recite his license plate number and he never recited it when he was issuing an order. About once or twice an hour the mayor would recite his license plate number.

The people had affectionately given him a nickname.

They called him General License Plate.

Headlines

"We are all Americans," was the way the President's broadcast started. "We are all brave people and loyal to America. We must stop spilling American blood, for it is too precious to be wasted. Its sacred energy must be used for the good of all Americans and the glory of this proud land."

etc.

The world press had a field day at America's expense.

The headline in *Pravda* said FRONTIER MISUNDER-STANDING.

Hsinhua (the official Chinese news agency) referred to the affair as "unfortunate but American."

Der Spiegel's headline was AN AMERICAN TRAGEDY.

The *London Times* said YANKS DO IT AGAIN.

Le Monde put forth the theory that perhaps it was a new American sport like football.

"Lay down your arms," the President said, nearing the

end of the broadcast. He concluded by saying, "Let us embrace together again, American embracing American, in the sight of almighty and forgiving God."

The townspeople responded with withering gunfire in the direction of anyplace they thought there might be a loudspeaker.

They took the surrender leaflets that were dropped on them by the thousands from low-flying aircraft and wiped their asses with them.

Siesta

What about the sombrero?

It easily adapted to the conditions of warfare, continuing to lie there in the street unnoticed by the town's inhabitants and miraculously safe from the martial activity going on around it.

Though millions of bullets and pieces of shrapnel and rockets and bombs were busy disturbing, killing and destroying everything in sight, the hat did not suffer a single scratch.

It just lay there totally undisturbed.

The temperature remained at zero.

The hat looked as if it were taking a siesta.

It was truly a sombrero for all seasons.

T_{ank}

The soldiers were amazed by Norman Mailer's courage as he was war-corresponding the rebellion. Again and again he exposed himself to tremendous concentrations of townspeople firepower.

He was with a tank outfit that tried to fight their way into the town but suffered hideous casualties as the result of anti-tank rockets that were in the possession of the town's crazed citizens.

Within a few moments after the attack was launched, there were nine tanks knocked out of action, some of them burning, and others just sitting there torn apart by a rocket, resting in the repose of tank death.

The tank that Norman Mailer was riding in was hit and two men were killed inside of it. Mailer and the rest of the crew climbed out. They were covered with blood from the dead men. All around them small arms fire was oxidizing the air. It was a very dangerous situation, but miraculously Mailer got out of it alive. He was interviewed by television newsmen a few moments after he got back. He was covered with so much blood that it looked as if he had been hit himself.

"What was it like?" was the first question Mailer was asked.

Later on that evening 100 million Americans saw Norman Mailer covered with blood say, "Hell. There is no other word for it. Hell."

Barbershop

Three days later the town was captured.

Over 6,000 people were dead inside of it, including 162 wounded children that were killed by a rocket that hit a temporary hospital in the basement of a public school.

The mayor, General License Plate, committed suicide rather than be captured. He shot himself in the heart but did not die immediately. He lived long enough afterwards to shout, "AZ 1492!"

Three of his comrades in arms stood there weeping.

There was a slight smile on the mayor's dead face.

"God-damn it," one of the men said.

Then they threw down their guns and put their hands up in the air and went out the front door of the barbershop that had been the headquarters for the defense of the town.

The mayor sat dead in a barber chair.

He had done his best.

It wasn't enough.
But still he was a brave man.
He had fought his hardest.
What else can you say?
He was an American.

Autograph

Even with thousands of Federal troops occupying the town and trying to create order out of insane havoc, nobody noticed the sombrero lying there in the street. Hundreds of vehicles: tanks, jeeps, trucks and armored personnel carriers passed up and down the street but not one of them touched the sombrero.

It remained undisturbed like a miracle in the center of the street as the town was occupied.

Though one interesting thing did occur when the last fighting was over, the temperature of the sombrero gradually returned to its original temperature when it dropped out of the sky just a few eventful days ago.

The temperature of the sombrero was now −24 again.

At one point Norman Mailer walked right by the sombrero but he didn't see it either. He stared at it for a couple of seconds and he might have seen it if it hadn't been for some soldiers who ran up to him, asking for his autograph.

Norman Mailer took his eyes off the sombrero and gave the soldiers their autographs.

"Thank you, Mr. Mailer," they said.

But Norman Mailer had looked away from the sombrero and he didn't look back again. He continued down the street to interview some of the townspeople who were being held prisoner in a movie theater.

He wanted to find out why in the hell they had taken on the entire United States Army.

He walked past the sombrero and did not see it.

Grandmother

None of the survivors were able to put together a coherent explanation about what had motivated them to riot and participate so bravely in such incredible carnage.

They just didn't know what had happened.

It was a mystery to them.

All they knew was that once they got started they couldn't stop.

The townspeople were of course now very contrite.

The survivors just shook their heads in confusion and weariness.

So many of them said, "I don't know what got into me," or "I've never done anything like this before."

They were grief-stricken over their own dead and wounded and the almost complete destruction of their town. They were also very sorry for all the people they had killed.

"I guess nothing one can say will ever make it right," said an old grandmother, who'd done her share of killing.

The colonel who was interrogating her had to stop the interrogation because she'd started crying.

"I've never done anything like this before," she said with tears flowing down her cheeks. "Oh, God," she said. "Oh, God."

The colonel stared awkwardly down at his feet.

He couldn't think of anything to say.

They hadn't taught him at West Point how to deal with situations like this. He had no experience.

He waited for her to stop crying.

The colonel looked up as Norman Mailer walked by.

Then he looked back at the old woman.

She was still crying.

The colonel looked down at his feet.

For a second he wondered why in the hell he had spent twenty years in the Army.

"Please, lady," he said.

The old woman looked a little like his grandmother.

It didn't work.

She continued crying.

Lincoln

Well, there you have it.

A week later the President of the United States came to the town and made his famous binding-the-wounds speech about Americans hand-in-hand walking into a brave and glorious future together, etc.

His speech was satellited all over the world and got a larger TV audience than the Super Bowl. Later on his speech would be reprinted in high school textbooks and would be referred to in the same terms as Lincoln's Gettysburg Address.

His most famous lines in the speech were, "We are on the edge of a great future together. Let us go hand-in-hand into that future with God's glory lighting the way like a torch and His mercy and forgiveness will be the path we walk on."

The town was declared a national monument and became quite a tourist attraction with the huge cemetery there being featured on millions of postcards.

The mayor, General License Plate, was proclaimed a hero, confused, yes, but still a hero and given an attractive burial plot in the cemetery with a marble statue of himself over the grave.

The first year the town was a national monument more people visited it than saw the Grand Canyon.

White

I guess the last remaining question is: What about the sombrero?

It's still there, lying in the street but its temperature had returned to -24 degrees and fortunately for America it stayed there.

Millions of tourists have walked all around it but not one of them has seen it, though it is in plain sight. How can you miss a very cold white sombrero lying in the Main Street of a town?

In other words: There is more to life than meets the eye.

*T*heater

In her dream Yukiko was only a block away
now from her friend's house in Seattle many years ago
while the American humorist continued firmly holding a
strand of her hair in his hand sixteen blocks away after
having lost it and then frantically searching for it like a
madman before calming down and applying logic to the
search and then finding it.

The rain had almost stopped in her dream.

It was misting now.

A cat was watching from the dry front porch of an old
house as she walked by. It was a very beautiful cat. Even
though the cat was sixty feet away, she could hear it
purring in her dream.

It's interesting, she thought in her dream, *that I can hear
that cat purring even though it's faraway*.

Then she took an omnipotent view of the dream. She

went from first person singular to third person. It was as if she were sitting in a theater, looking at a movie of her dream.

I must be dreaming, she thought, *because it's impossible to hear a cat purring from that distance*. So she became more and more aware that she was dreaming the dream and it began to change in color and vividness. The dream became slightly washed out and overexposed.

The dominant theme became the sound of the cat purring. It grew louder and louder until it sounded like a gentle chain saw. Then her father who was alive and everything that you couldn't see in the dream changed into being dead. He was dead now but you still couldn't see him.

His death was now everything that you couldn't see in the dream, but it didn't make her unhappy. His death was just there. It was a fact.

The purring of the cat was what interested her the most. She couldn't figure out why it was so loud and that she could hear it purring all the way from the porch.

So night continued passing while Yukiko dreamt on, with her long hair reflecting darkness like a mirror.

*J*apan

It was now 11:15.

The American humorist decided that he wanted to listen to some music while he sat there holding the strand of Japanese hair in his hand. He got up with the Japanese hair in one hand and went over and turned on the radio.

The room was suddenly filled with the sound of Country and Western music. He liked C and W music. It was his favorite music. He went back and sat down on the couch and listened to songs about heartbreak and truck driving while he held his Japanese hair.

He wondered if there had ever been a Country and Western song written about loving a Japanese woman. He didn't think so. It was an unlikely theme for a C and W song. *Maybe I should write one*, he thought, and then started working on the song in his mind:

"She's my little lady from Japan
and I love her as much as I can.
Her hair is black and her skin is like moonlight.
I love to put my arms around her and hold her tight."

As he wrote the song in his mind, he imagined Waylon Jennings singing it on the Grand Ole Opry:

"She's from a faraway land.
She's my little lady from Japan.
Her dark eyes are all the mysteries of the East
and everytime I look into them I have a feast."

Waylon Jennings did a great job of singing the song and he also recorded it and the song became the number one hit in the country. You could hear it in every bar and café in America and everywhere that people listened to Country and Western music. It owned the air.

He started singing the song aloud to himself:

"She's my little lady from Japan,"
holding one long strand of black hair in his hand.

DATE DUE

9 Dec 76			
FEB 2 8 1978			
AUG 8 1978			
APR - 8 1980			
SE 29 '80			
JA 26 '81			
NO 23 '83